Maureen Birnbaum, Barbarian Swordsperson

Maureen Birnbaum, Barbarian Swordsperson

by

**George
Alec
Effinger**

This book is in memory of Mimi,
who looked forward to reading the last story.

MAUREEN BIRNBAUM,
BARBARIAN SWORDSPERSON

"Maureen Birnbaum, Barbarian Swordsperson" was first published in *The Magazine of Fantasy and Science Fiction,* January, '82. Reprinted by permission of the author.
"Maureen Birnbaum at the Earth's Core" was first published in *The Magazine of Fantasy and Science Fiction,* January, '86. Reprinted by permission of the author.
"Maureen Birnbaum on the Art of War" was first published in *Friends of the Horseclans,* edited by Robert Adams, © 1987. Reprinted by permission of the author.
"Maureen Birnbaum After Dark" was first published in *Foundations Friends,* edited by Martin Harry Greenberg, © 1989. Reprinted by permission of the author.
"Maureen Birnbaum Goes Shopynge" was first published in *The Fantastic Adventures of Robin Hood,* edited by Martin Harry Greenberg, © 1991. Reprinted by permission of the author.
"Maureen Birnbaum at the Looming Awfulness" was written especially for this volume. First published in *Maureen Birnbaum, Barbarian Swordsperson: The Complete Adventures,* June 1993. Copyright © 1993, by George Alec Effinger. Printed by permission of the author.
"Maureen Birnbaum's Lunar Adventure," is revised from an earlier version, and is printed by permission of the author. Copyright © 1993, by George Alec Effinger.

ISBN 1-56865-101-5

PRINTED IN THE UNITED STATES OF AMERICA

Maureen Birnbaum,
Barbarian
Swordsperson

CONTENTS

A Few Words from Muffy Birnbaum's Most Passionate Admirer

by Mike Resnick

The first time I encountered Maureen Birnbaum was in 1985, at an obscure little convention in New Orleans known as Deltacon. There were only three professional writers in attendance: I was the Guest of Honor, flown in from Ohio, and George Alec Effinger and Jo Clayton, who has since migrated to Oregon, were the local writers.

We had each been asked to read from our works, but this was not the utmost in literary conventions, and people from the committee kept coming up to us to ask if we would postpone the readings for another hour or so while they re-ran yet another episode of *Blake's 7*. As I recall, somewhere around ten at night, we got tired of waiting, found a small room in the hotel, and each of us read to the other two.

Jo read something serious and moving. I quite forget what I read. And then George began reading "Maureen Birnbaum at the Earth's Core," and for the first time in my life I quite literally fell out of my chair laughing. It was not only hilarious in its own right; it was not only brilliant as a parody of Edgar Rice Burroughs' Pellucidar stories; but it also created an entirely new type of humor—Preppy Science Fiction.

How long had this been going on, I wanted to know. George replied that this was the second story, the first having been "Maureen Birnbaum, Barbarian Swordsperson," which he had not brought with him. Only the fact that I was staying in New Orleans a few extra days and would be able to borrow a copy later in the week prevented me from renting a car and driving to George's apartment that night to read it—and from that day to this, I have been Muffy Birnbaum's Number One Fan.

I even had something to do, that week, with the publication of the book you are holding in your hands. I convinced George that Muffy's future adventures should average 10,000 words apiece, rather than the paltry 4,000 of her first adventure. It was entirely selfish; I couldn't bear to wait until the turn of the century for enough Birnbaum wordage to exist for someone to think of collecting the stories in book form.

Then I settled back—impatiently—to await more Muffy stories. Having done pretty much all she could to destroy a pair of old Edgar's paradises, she next appeared in the world of Bob Adams' Horseclans. Then, to prove she wasn't limited to multi-volume adventure worlds, she turned up in the world of Isaac Asimov's "Nightfall."

By this time, most of the practicing science fiction writers were practically begging George to send Muffy to *their* worlds next, but George fooled them all by sending her to Sherwood Forest instead. (In fact, that was the Resnick Family's second contribution to Muffy's mythos. George and I were collaborating with Jack Chalker on *The Red Tape War* at the time, and George remarked to me over the phone that his deadline on sending Muffy into Robin Hood's world was drawing close and he still hadn't come up with an idea; Carol overheard my end of the conversation and suggested a shop-off between Muffy and Maid Marian. George clutched at the straw and within a few days had turned it into pure gold.)

Since then she has also gone after the Holy Grail, entered Lovecraft's world of Looming Awfulness, and out-Feghooted the redoubtable Ferdinand—and while that brings Volume One to a close, there are too many Muffy Birnbaum fans out there (to say nothing of the ravening hordes of Bitsy Spiegelman *aficionados*) to allow George to stop bringing these tales to a waiting world. For one thing, Muffy has yet to visit Kirinyaga, so you know *I* won't let him quit.

George has written these stories with such facility that I have a feeling most people don't begin to realize the work that goes into them. I know, for example, that he spent more than a month immersing himself in Horseclans books before writing the first word of "Maureen Birnbaum on the Art of War," and that is typical of the research that goes into these little gems.

Most people don't realize, either, just what an accomplishment *selling* them was. Humor is a very subjective thing, probably the hardest fictional commodity to sell. I take an enormous pride in the fact that I have placed all 33 of Lucifer Jones's adventures, exploits and encounters with *Pulphouse Magazine*—but they all sold to the same editor, who happened to be a diehard Lucifer fan. George, on the other hand, after selling the first two Muffy stories to Ed Ferman of the *Magazine of Fantasy and Science Fiction,* had to please a different editor every single time out of the box; you really don't know how difficult that is with humor until you've tried it. (In fact, a case can be made that the one thing Ed Ferman, Isaac Asimov, Bob Adams, Richard Gilliam, Ed Kramer and Martin H. Greenberg have in common is that they all fell hopelessly in love with Muffy.)

George has accomplished a hell of a lot in his career. The Marid novels— *When Gravity Fails, A Fire in the Sun, The Exile Kiss*—are quite possibly the most important series to come out of science fiction in the last couple of decades. Sandor Courane, the science fiction writer/editor who has died in at least a dozen stories and keeps coming back in the sequels, is unique in the history of the genre. George is also the absolute master of the science fiction sports story.

But I'll tell you something: the Birnbaum stories are written with such wit, such style, such pure *love* for the field, that I, for one, won't be surprised if Muffy outlives all of George's other creations.

And when Volume Two comes out in a few years, I'll be right back here to smugly remind you that I was right.

I'm often asked where the character of Maureen Birnbaum came from. The glib reply is that I was sitting in a college hangout called Fat Harry's one afternoon. I was working over a few pages I'd written that day, and enjoying a good cheeseburger, fries, and large Coke (Nature's perfect meal). At a table near me were four Tulane co-eds who were talking just loud enough for me to catch every word. To make a dull but true story short, each of them was an ideal model for Muffy. The conversation ran the entire emotional gamut from sweaters to—God forbid—Peter Pan collars. And they spoke in frequent *italics.* You could just hear them chiming.

All I've done is to take one of those college girls, put a broadsword in her hands, and maroon her in the familiar milieus of some of my favorite SF authors. At last the fantasy and science fiction field has a heroine who can truly shop her way out of a paper bag. I am quietly humble about this achievement.

This first story takes Muffy to a place Very Much Like the planet B*RS**M, created by Edgar Rice Burroughs.

Maureen Birnbaum,
Barbarian Swordsperson

Maureen Birnbaum, Barbarian Swordsperson

by Bitsy Spiegelman

(as told to George Alec Effinger)

THE LAST TIME I saw Muffy Birnbaum was, let me see, last December—no, make that last January, because it was right after exams and before Mums and I spent a couple of dreadful weeks at the B and T in Palm Beach. So that makes it ten months almost, and she told me to wait a year before I revealed this to the world, to use her exact words. But I don't think Muffy will mind that I'm two months early. She's long ago and far away, if you believe her story. Do I believe her story? Look. She was missing for a full week, and then I get this telegram—a telegram, can you believe it? Not a phone call. Meet me under the Clock, 15 January, noonish. Come alone. Trust me. Kisses, Muffy. What was I supposed to think? I show up and she's not there, but there's a note waiting for me: Come to Room 1623. Just too mysterious, but up I go. The door's open and I walk in, and there's goddamn Maureen Danielle Birnbaum practically naked, wearing nothing but these leather straps across her shoulders and a little gold G-string, and she's got this goddamned sword in one hand like she was expecting the Sheriff of Nottingham or something to come through the door instead of her best friend and roommate. I couldn't think of anything to say at first, so she called down for some ice, pointed to a chair, and began to *tell me this story. I'll give it to you just the way it is on my tape; then you can tell me if you believe it.*

S O LISTEN, I'm telling you this story. Believe me, I'd *had* it, absolutely *had* it. School was a complete bore and I was absolutely falling to pieces. Absolutely. I needed a vacation and I told Daddy that a little skiing action would shape me up very nicely, and so just like that, I found myself at Mad River Glen, looking very neat, I thought, until I saw some of the competition, the collegiate talent. They were deadly cut and they knew it, and all you had to do was ask and they'd tell you all about it. You could just about tell where they went to school, like they were wearing uniforms. The Vassar girls were the ones sort of flouncing downhill wearing their circle pins on the front of their hundred-dollar goose-down ski parkas. The Bennington girls were the ones looking rugged and trying to ski back *uphill.* Definitely Not Our Kind, sweetie.

Are those your cigarettes, Bitsy? Mind if I—no, just toss me the whole pack. I have matches here in the ashtray. My *God.* I haven't had a cigarette in so *long*—

Where was I? Vermont, right. So I was staring down this goddamn hill, if you can believe it, and I'm all set to push off and go barreling down the mountain at some outrageous speed, when I stop. I look up at the sky—it's starting to get dark, you know, and absolutely clear and kind of sweet, but *cold*—when I feel this weird feeling inside. First I thought I was going to *die,* just absolutely die. Then I thought, "My God, I know what it is. And they always say nothing can happen if—" You know. But I was wrong both times. The next thing I knew I was standing stark naked in the snow beside my body, which was still dressed in this cute outfit from L. L. Bean, and I thought, "Muffy, you've had it." I thought I was dead or something, but I didn't understand why I was so goddamn *cold.* Then I looked up into the sky and this bright red dot caught my eye and I sort of shivered. I knew right then, I said to myself, "That is where I'm going." Heaven or Hell, here I come. And just like that I felt this whooshing and dizziness and everything, and I opened my eyes, and I wasn't in Vermont anymore, but I was still cold.

I'm drinking Bloody Marys. It isn't too early for you, is it? Then you try calling down for ice, I've given up on them. Are you hungry? We'll have lunch later. I'm putting myself on a diet, but I'll go with you and you can have something.

Anyway, they didn't prepare me at the Greenberg School for what was waiting for me when I opened my eyes. Here I was on some weirdo planet out in space, for God's sake. Say, Bitsy, do you have any gum or what? Chiclets? Yuck. Let me have—no, just one. Thanks. A weirdo planet, if you can believe that. I was standing there at the top of the run one second, having this *unbelievable* fight with the zipper on the jacket Pammy—that's Daddy's second wife—bought me for Christmas, and the next minute I'm up to my ankles in orange grunge. And I was so cold I thought I would freeze to death. I was cold because—we're just going to have to live without the ice, I think, Bitsy, because this hotel probably has a goddamn *policy* against it or something, so just pour it in the glass—I was standing there in the proverbial buff! Me! Three years living with me at the Greenberg School, and even you never saw my pink little derriere. And here I am starko for the whole world to see. What world it was I didn't know, so I didn't know *who* could see, but believe me, Bitsy, I didn't particularly care. Right then I had two or three pressing problems on my mind, and getting dressed was high on the list. I really missed that ski outfit. It was cold as hell.

All around me there was nothing but this gross orange stuff on the ground. I don't know what it was. It wasn't grass, I know that. It felt more like the kind of sponge the cleaning woman keeps under your sink for a couple of years. Gross. And there was nothing else to see except some low hills off in one direction. I decided to head that way. There sure wasn't anything the other way, and—who knew?—there may have been a Bloomingdale's on the other side of the hills. At that point I would have settled for Lamston's, *believe* me.

You're going to die laughing when I tell you this, absolutely die. When I took a step I went sailing up into the air. Just like a balloon, and I thought, "Muffy, honey, *what* did they put in your *beer?*" When I settled back down, I tried it again, and I flew away again. It took me absolutely an hour to figure out how to walk and run and all that. I still don't know why it was. One of those lame boys from Brush-Bennett would know, right off the bat, but it wasn't all that important to me. I just needed to learn to handle it. So in a while, still freezing my completely cute buns off, I got to the top of the first hill and I looked down at my new world.

You want to know what I saw? Was that the door? You better get it, Bitsy, because even though Daddy stays here *all* the time, the staff has been just too dreary for words. You should have heard what they said about my sword. They talked about my sword a lot, because they were too embarrassed to mention my costume. I think it's—who? The ice? Would you be a dear and leave the boy something? I don't have a goddamned *penny*. I mean, you don't see any pockets, do you?

There was more orange crud all the way to the whatyoucall—the horizon. But there was a little crowd of people down there about a quarter of a mile away. It looked to me like a little tailgate party, like we used to have with your parents in New Haven before the Harvard game. I thought, "That's nice, they'll be able to drive me to a decent motel or something until I can get settled." But then I wondered how I was going to walk up to them all naked and glowing with health and frostbite and all. I thought about covering up the more strategic areas with the orange stuff from the ground, but I didn't even know if I could rip it loose. I was standing there thinking when I heard this girl scream. She sounded like Corkie the time we threw the dead fish into the shower with her. There was something *awful* going on down there, a mugging or a purse-snatching or something terrible, so what does yours truly do? I started running downhill toward them. Don't look so *surprised*. It's just something you do when you find yourself on a creepy planet, undressed and stone cold, with nothing else around except the two moons in the sky. Did I mention that there were two moons? Well, there were. I ran toward the people below because I needed a lift into town, wherever it was, and if I helped the poor girl out maybe her daddy would let me stay at their place for a while.

When I got closer I saw that I had made just a little bitty mistake. The station wagon and the Yalies turned into a drastic and severe kind of a fight, a brawl, really, except everybody was using one of these swords and they were using them for *real*. I mean, Bitsy, my *God*, blood was pouring all over *everywhere* and people were actually *dying* and it was all kind of heroic and all that and very horrible and dramatic. It was people against big, giant things with four arms. No, really. Really. Bitsy, stop *laughing*. There were these huge old creatures with four arms, and they were chopping away at these normal-sized people, with everybody fighting away with these *intense* grins on their faces. I never did figure out about that, why they were all *smiling* while they were whacking away at each other. Anyway, while I stood there the two groups just about wiped each other out, all the giant creatures except one and all the people except this one positively *devastating* guy. All the other guys and girls were lying very dead on the orange stuff, and it wasn't really *surprising*. I mean, just imagine something that's twelve feet tall and has arms slashing swords around up where you can barely see, for God's sake. And then this *darling* boy goes and tangles his adorable legs and falls over backwards.

Bitsy, are you listening to this, or what? I mean, I don't know why I even bothered—no, look. I didn't *have* to send you the telegram. I could have called Mother. Except she would have had *kittens* if she had seen me like this. Do you understand? This was a very moving moment for me, Bitsy, I mean, watching these kids fighting like that and all, and even though I didn't know them, I got very emotional and everything. So I'd appreciate it, I really would, if you'd show a little respect. You've never had to fight for *anything* except with the burger-brained Amherst freshman you went out with senior year. Of *course* I remember him. He reminds me a lot of these four-armed things.

Well, if anything *terminal* happened to my blond hero, that monster was coming after *me* next. So, perky little thing that I am, I run up and grab a sword—this sword, I call her "Old Betsy" because that's what Davy Crockett called his rifle or something—I grab Old Betsy and I stand there trying not to look that . . . thing in the eye. This was very easy, believe me, because his eyes are *at least* six feet over my head. And I'm all nice and balanced—*you* remember, you were there, you remember how *tremendous* I was in that six weeks of fencing we had sophomore year, with what's-her-name, Miss Duplante? You remember how she was absolutely terrified of me? Anyway, picture me standing there *en garde* waiting for this four-armed darling to settle into position. But he *doesn't*, that's what's so scary, he just goes *whacko!* and takes a swipe at my goddamn head.

Only I'm not there anymore, I'm about fifty feet away. I remembered that I could jump, but *really*. So I hop around for a minute or two to get my bearings and to stay away from the thing's sword. I hop, and I jump, bounce, bounce, bounce, all around the landscape. And the creature is watching me, *mad as hell*. My blond dream is still on the ground, and he's watching, too. "Get a *sword*, dummy," I yell at him, and he nods. That's something else I forgot to tell you, Bitsy. All the people on this planet speak English. It's really neat and very convenient. So between the two of us we finished the monster off. No, it's just too *awful* to think about, stabbing and bleeding and hacking and all like that. Fencing was a lot tidier—you know, just a kind of polite poking around with a sharp stick. And *I* had to do all the *heavyweight* hacking because my boyfriend couldn't reach anything terribly vital on the four-armed thing. He was taking mighty swings at the

11

giant's knees, and meanwhile good old Muffy is cutting its pathetic head off. Just altogether *unreal.*

Well, that's the dynamic, exciting carnage part. After I took care of the immediate danger, the boy starts to talk to me. "Hello," he goes. "You were excellent."

"Thanks," I go. At this point I feel like I'm riding on a horse with only one rocker, but I don't let it show. The old Greenberg School *pride,* Bitsy.

He goes, "My name is Prince Van."

"Uh-huh," I go. "I'm Maureen Birnbaum. My daddy is a contract lawyer and I live with my mother. We raise golden retrievers."

"How nice," the prince goes. Let me tell you what this guy *looked* like! You wouldn't *believe* it! Do you remember that boy who came down to visit that drecky redhead from Staten Island? No, not the boy from Rutgers, the one from—where was it? That place I never *heard* of—Colby College, in Maine? Sounds like a goddamned *cheese* factory or something? Anyway, standing beside me on the orange stuff is something just like him, only the prince is awesome. He is strong and blond with perfect teeth and eyes like Paul Newman and he's wearing, well, you see what I'm wearing. Just *imagine,* honey, if that isn't just too devastating for you. He is *beautiful.* And his name is Prince Van. I always told you that someday my prince would—

Okay, okay. I didn't really know what to say to him or anything. I mean, we'd just had this sort of pitched battle and all, and there were all these unpleasant *bodies* laying around—we were stepping over people here and there, and I was trying not to notice. We stopped and he bent down and took this harness for me from someone he said had been his sister. He didn't seem sad or anything. He was very brave, *intensely* brave, no tears for Sis, the gang back at the palace wouldn't approve. And all the dead boys looked just like him, all blond and large and uncomfortably cute, and all the girls looked just like Tri-Delts, with feathered blond hair and perfect teeth. They had been his retinue, Prince Van explained, and he said I shouldn't grieve. He could get another one.

"Where to?" I go. The palace couldn't be too far away, I thought.

"Well," he says—and his voice is like a handful of Valium; I just wanted to curl up and listen to it—he says, like, "my city is two thousand miles *that* way," he pointed, "but there is a closer city one thousand miles that way." He pointed behind us.

I go, *"Thousand?* You've got to be kidding."

He says, like, "I have never seen anyone like you." And he smiled. Bitsy,

12

that was just the kind of thing my mother had *warned* me about, and I had begun to think it didn't really exist. I think I was in love.

"I'm from another world," I go. I tried to sound like I partied around in space quite a bit.

"That explains it," he goes. "It explains your strength and agility and your exotic beauty. I am captivated by your raven tresses. No one on our world has hair your color. It is very beautiful." *Raven tresses*, for God's sake! I think I blushed, and I think he wanted me to. We were holding hands by now. I was thinking about one or two thousand miles alone with Prince Van of Who-Knows-Where. I wondered what boys and girls did on this planet when they were alone. I decided that it was the same everywhere.

We walked for a long time and I asked a lot of questions. He must have thought I was just *really* lame, but he never laughed at me. I learned that the cities are so far because we were walking across the bottom of what had been a great ocean, years and years before. There weren't oceans and lakes and things on this planet now. They have all their water delivered or something. I thought, "There's *oil* down there." I wanted to remember that for when we got to the palace. I don't think anyone had realized it yet.

"Then where do you go sailing?" I go.

"Sailing?" he asked innocently.

"What about swimming?"

"Swimming?"

He was cute, absolutely *tremendous*, in fact, but life without sailing and swimming would be just too terribly *triste*, you know? And I think he was just being polite before when I mentioned golden retrievers.

I say, like, "Is there somewhere I can pick up some clothes?" I figured that although his city was two thousand miles away, there were probably isolated little ocean-bottom suburbs along the way or shopping malls where all the blond people came to buy new straps and swords and stuff.

"Clothes?" he goes. I knew he was going to say that, I just knew it, but as gross as it was, I had to hear it from his own lips.

I walked along for a while, *dying*, absolutely dying for a cigarette, not saying anything. Then I couldn't stand it any longer. "Van," I go, "listen. It isn't like it hasn't been wonderful with you, cutting up that big old monster and all. But, like, there are some things about this relationship that are totally the worst, but *really*."

"Relationship?" he goes. He kept smiling. I think I could eventually see enough of it.

13

I explained it all to him. There were no horses. There was no sailing, no swimming, no skiing, no racquetball. There were no penny loafers, no mixers at the boy's schools, no yearbooks. There was no Junior Year Abroad, no Franny and Zooey Glass, no Nantucket Island, no *Coors*. There was no Sunday *Times*, no Godiva chocolates, no Dustin Hoffman. There was no Joni Mitchell and no food processors and no golden retrievers and no little green Triumphs.

There were no clothes. Bitsy, *there was no shopping!*

So kind of sadly, I kissed him on the cheek and told myself that his couldn't-be-cuter expression was a little sad, too. I say, like, *"Adieu, mon cher,"* and I give him a little wave. Then I stretched myself out toward the sky again—oh, yes, just a little late I told myself that I wasn't absolutely sure about what I was doing, that I might end up God knows where—and waited to whoosh back to the snowy mountaintop in Vermont. I missed. But fortunately it wasn't as bad as it could have been. I mean, I didn't land on *Saturn* or anything. I turned up on the corner of Eighth Avenue and 45th Street. No one noticed me very much; I fit right into that neighborhood.

So if I can just ask you a little favor, Bitsy, then I'll be on my way. Yes, on my way, goddamn it, I'm going back. I'm not going to leave that but totally attractive Prince Van to those perky blonde hometown honeys—he is *mine*. I kept my harness and Old Betsy on the way here, so I think I know how to get back there again with anything I want to take with me. So I want to pick up a few things first. My daddy always told me to Be Prepared. He said that all the time, he's a Mason or something. He sure was prepared when he met Pammy and he's close to fifty years old.

Never mind. Anyway, let's go rummage in a bin somewhere and suit me up with a plaid skirt or two and some cute jeans and some sweaters and some alligator shirts and Top-siders and a brand-new insulated ski jacket and sunglasses and some *Je Reviens* and stuff. It'll be fun!

Oh. And a circle pin. My old one wore out.

WE WENT SHOPPING *at Saks and Bloomingdale's—I went to Korvettes and got her some cheaper clothes first, though. I didn't want to walk around Manhattan with Muffy while she was wearing nothing but suspenders and no pants. We charged four hundred dollars to Mums' cards, and let me tell you I heard about that a few weeks later. But I was sworn to secrecy. Now Muffy's gone again,*

14

back to her secret paradise in the sky, back to Prince Van of the terribly straight teeth. I hope she's happy. I hope she comes back some day to tell me her adventures. I hope she pays me back the four hundred dollars. Perhaps only time will tell. . . .

15

I figured that if one Edgar Rice Burroughs world was good, two would be even better, so I craftily devised a way to send poor, suffering Muffy to P*LL*C*D*R, at the Center of the Earth. Here she acquires Many Things, including her warrior-woman costume and, though she doesn't realize it at the time, the true Love of Her Life.

Maureen Birnbaum
at the Earth's Core

Maureen Birnbaum at the Earth's Core

by Bitsy Spiegelman

(as told to George Alec Effinger)

ALL I KNOW *is that I was supposed to leave for Cancún. The plane was at two, and you know what traffic is like in the sleet to the airport, so I was planning to leave the apartment sometime around noon to get there and get my bags checked through and have enough time to pour three or four drinks into me. I do not like to fly—it doesn't matter if the plane is coming down in Aspen or Cancún or Oz. I do not like to fly. The four drinks wouldn't calm me either, unless they were washing down five of the big Valiums. The baby blue ones. Whatever they are. Tens. I think.*

Anyway, I'd packed two days before and checked everything at least twice, had my passport and my tickets in my purse with cab fare in case my sweet little RX-7 perished heroically somewhere on the Brooklyn-Queens Expressway, and I was all set to start hauling my bags out to the car, when guess what? The phone rang. My mother, I figured. It's always my mother. Mums would be calling to let me know the latest herpes statistics or something, so I just let it ring. It rang and rang and rang. I had all the luggage in the car, and the goddamn telephone was still ringing. Mums only rings ten times. So I answered it. I go "Hello?" And I was in a real rush because I had

19

only two hours to get maybe twelve miles on the best highway system in the Free World.

"*Bitsy?*" goes this girl's voice.

"Look, I really have to run. Got to catch a plane. Call me next week, we'll have lunch."

"*Bitsy? This is Maureen. Muffy.*"

I could have died just standing there with the phone against my ear. It was Maureen Birnbaum, giving me a little call on January 15, 1985, exactly four years to the day since she had last disappeared. I didn't know what to say to her for a moment. "Muffy," I managed at last, "you still owe my mother four hundred dollars."

"I meant to talk to you about that. Can I see you? It's awfully important, I mean really."

Four years ago she'd shown up in midtown Manhattan wearing a couple of square inches of gold lamé and carrying an honest-to-God sword. She'd just gotten back from Mars, you see. After she gave me her absolutely incredible story, she'd vanished for four solid years without so much as a note or card. Now she wanted to catch up on old times and tell me more about Mars and stuff and the beautiful prince she'd fallen in love with. "Listen, Muffy," I go, "it would be like, great, except I was just going out the door. Club Med, you know. I've saved up all year for this, okay?"

"*Bitsy.*" There was this creepiness in her voice that she'd get sometimes when we were roommates back at the Greenberg School, whenever I suggested—in a kind and thoughtful way, I mean—that she might be putting on a little heftiness, hip-wise.

It was a traumatic moment for me. I felt this dreadful sinking feeling. What could I do?

I'll tell you what I did: I went to Cancún, met a dentist from Boston with a face you'd claw your way to get up close to, had a pretty neat time broiling on the sand there with him for a week, found out the last day that he was married, got a couple of little tchatchkes to remember him by because he was feeling so impure and all, and came home. There was a cassette tape sitting on Mums's copy of an Erma Bombeck book she'd lent me to make me feel even guiltier about being her child. I played the tape. Just like that last time, you have your choice of believing any of this or not. A lot I care.

BITSY? Bitsy, how do you start—is it running? Is this, like, working? Let me run it back—
It's working. Great. So how the *hell* are you, sweetie? I hope you're having a really cruddy time in Mexico, because I went through absolute hell to see you, and you leave me to toast your buns in the sun.

The last time you saw me, I had on my new clothes and all the rest were packed in the Louis Vuitton bag. I planned to stay in the hotel until about midnight; then I was going to sneak outside, look up in the sky and find Mars, raise my supple, beseeching, cashmere-clad arms to the God of War, and whoosh my way back to Prince Van. I had already figured out how I was going to play him: vivacious, exciting, yet, you know, *cool*. I'll never forget that gaggy feeling I got when I found out that people on Mars don't know what a *relationship* is. I was going to have to teach them. I mean *him*. The rest of them could go on living like animals—I should worry?

Ten o'clock, eleven o'clock—I had a glass of white wine in the bar and talked with this so-so guy who said he was a production assistant; but he wouldn't ever come out and tell me exactly what he assisted producing. About a quarter to midnight, I flashed him my Number Three smile— Glamorous But Not Inviting—and told him I had to powder my nose. I raced back up to the room, grabbed my bag, and hurried back down to the lobby. It was right then that I realized I didn't have Dime One left over to pay the bill, so I kissed it off and kept the key. They'll either charge Daddy or God will send me to hell, ha ha.

I realized that I couldn't see much of the sky from that part of town, and the only open place I could think of was Central Park. That's cute, isn't it? Maureen Birnbaum, the Marie Osmond of Long Island, walking alone into the treacherous wastes of Central Park at midnight. Alone, but not unarmed —see, I still had Old Betsy, and if any mugger in that park tried anything funny with me, he'd come home from work with one or two important parts hacked off his goddamn body.

So Central Park it had to be. Except—can you believe it?—it was raining. I mean, *pouring*. You couldn't see the top of the Empire State Building, let alone Mars. Oh, fudge, I said to myself, and I went back into the hotel. I took my bag up to the room, then came back down to the bar and let the production assistant buy me a drink. I told the bartender I wanted a pina colada, and he goes, "A what?" Like he'd never heard it before or nobody drank them anymore. He gave me a look like I was from another planet or something. Well, of course, I *did* just get back from another planet; but that wasn't really any reason for this measly bartender to make me feel like a social leper, for God's sake. He smirked to himself like I'd ordered some kind of drink that you hear about only in works of literature, like a martini or a mint julep or something. And then he goes, "I'm sorry, miss, but we took all the disco off the jukebox a long time ago." And the production assistant thought that was pretty funny, too. Then he had the nerve—the prod. ass., I mean—to suggest we go someplace else, *in the Bronx yet!* So I told him I had to get up early because I was going to donate a kidney, and went to my room and watched TV.

There is nothing more boring *in the whole world* than killing time. The whole next day I might as well have been socked in at some airport or something, because getting to Mars was going to have to wait until after dark. I tried a little window shopping, but how much fun is that when you don't have any cash and all your credit cards are probably lying in an abandoned ski suit somewhere in Vermont? I mean, even if you don't intend to spend money, you spend money—it's a law of nature or something. When you know you absolutely, positively *can't*, well, it's like running out of gas in the dark, romantic woods late at night with Father Flanagan. I mean, why *torture* yourself, you know?

I called Daddy, but he and Pammy were out of town too, I remembered. They went to St. Croix when they sent me to Mad River Glen. I'd been to Mars and back, but they were probably still down in the sun and fun. I was all alone. I was penniless. I was beginning to feel like I'd accidentally been erased by the Big Computer or something. So I watched more TV and sent down to room service for food and put it on the bill.

I didn't wait for midnight. I went out about seven o'clock when it got dark, and it wasn't raining! Hooray! A point for me. I looked up in the sky, and I saw maybe three stars. That's all. People in New York don't realize there're a whole lot of stars they're missing out on. New York kids must be scared out of their punky, wiseass little minds if they ever get out into the country and look up at the night sky. "Hey, what the hell are *those?*" they go. "Stars," somebody tells 'em. "Nuh-uh. How come we don't got that many on 125th Street?" they go. "Because that's God punishing you for covering all the subway cars with spray paint."

I have become aware of social problems, Bitsy, believe it or not. You'll hear all about it. In the past four years I've learned a lot about right and wrong. I'm dead set against certain things now. For one, I'm not Muffy anymore. No, no way, Monet. I'm Maureen and I'm proud of it. Maureen's

22

my name, my real name. Muffy was my slave name. It's what all those Columbia math majors called me. No more, kiddo.

And you've changed a little, too, haven't you? I looked around for something to drink—no vodka, no rum, no tequila. That's not the old Blitzy-Bitsy Spiegelman I remember. A little new Beaujolais in the kitchen and some classy-looking whites—you've been reading those *magazines* again, honey. And that picture on the table—*Bitsy!* For crying out loud, do you realize you've cut your hair exactly the same way as my mother's *Lhasa apso?* And what's with the funky, stretched-out sweatshirt hanging off your shoulder? You look like you can't afford your own clothes and have to raid Goodwill boxes at night. Times change, I guess. From looking around, I think I want to get out of here *real* fast. But, as your mother says, "As long as you've got your health." I notice you don't have the Captain and Tenille records I gave you anymore. The Knack and Shaun Cassidy albums are missing, too; now there are a few *black faces* peeping out of your stereo cabinet. Why Bitsy, how sophisticated of you! Our tastes just keep on broadening, don't they? Is the kid with sunglasses and the glittery glove the one who sings with his brothers? He still doesn't look old enough to be let out by himself. I mean, his voice hasn't changed or anything.

Where was I? Oh, yeah. Well, I went to Central Park and looked for the darkest, loneliest place I could find. I don't know, maybe it was the sight of me with my genuine leather bag in one hand and a long jeweled sword in the other, but nobody bothered me. Somewhere around Sixty-eighth Street I looked up into the sky again. There were more stars here—about six more. I hoped one of those dots of light was Mars. I clutched my bag and my sword, closed my eyes tighty-tight, and projected myself headlong into space. It's a trick you learn. The first time is just an accident, but then you stumble on how to do it whenever you want. You just sort of throw yourself across this creepy-cold distance between Earth and, like, wherever.

Steering is another matter entirely, honey, let me tell you. Forget what they've told you, it's *not* all in the wrist. I mean, when I tried to get from Mars to Vermont, I ended up in Manhattan. This time, trying to whoosh myself back to Mars, I ended up—

You're not going to believe this—

I landed inside the hollow Earth.

Don't ask me how I could aim at the sky and land five hundred miles below the dead brown grass of Central Park. I'm not sure. And you're going to have to forget (if you haven't already) all about Mr. Reuven's lectures about the Earth's crust and the mantle and the molten core and so on and

on. I knew I was *inside,* because there was rock all around and above me
where the sky should be, and the far, hazy distances lifted up to meet the
roof. Overhead there was some kind of blazing little sun that never went
out—it was always daytime—but it was the kind of light that makes you
look like you've been dead for a week. It wasn't like real sunlight. I was
there for four years and I didn't get the beginning of a tan, even though I
didn't wear any more clothes than I did on Mars.

I was in the middle of a big forest—a jungle, really, and the trees were
covered with hanging vines and bright, beautiful flowers climbing the
trunks. Orchids, I think, though they were shaped funny and were strange
colors. Everything in this place was shaped funny, I came to realize, and
was a funny color. I wandered around in the jungle for a little while, just
staring at the birds and monkeys and butterflies and flowers. It was hot. Let
me tell you, it was as hot as your mother's apartment was that Fourth of
July when your A. C. went out and you couldn't get anybody to come fix it
on the holiday. I was sweating the proverbial bullets. I said to myself, I go
"Muffy"—see, I wasn't socially aware yet; it took four years of suffering and
hardship to teach me those lessons—I go "Muffy, you know what would be
nice? Let's change into something a little cooler." I had in mind a pair of
khaki shorts and a Ralph Lauren polo shirt and my old Tretorn tennis
sneaks. So I opened my suitcase and took off my winter stuff—you have to
picture this in your mind, Bitsy, step-by-step—and I was rummaging
around, looking for the right outfit, when out from behind this tree stepped
this ape.

Well, I screamed. *You'd* scream, too. I was naked. I'd never *been* naked
in front of an ape before.

He galumphed toward me with his knuckles on the ground, carrying
some dead animal in his mouth. Behind him came maybe twenty more
apes. I told myself not to be terrified; I'd faced bigger monsters on Mars,
and these huge old monkeys were probably just as scared of me as I was of
them. That's what they always say on TV. Marlin Perkins is always going
like, "These huge old monkeys of the deep jungle look fearsome, but in
truth they are gentle browsers and vegetarians." Then I thought, why the
hell does it have this dead *thing* in its mouth if it's a vegetarian?

I stood very still, wishing I could reach down and pick up my sword, Old
Betsy, but I didn't dare move. The big ape came right up to me and
stopped. He stared at me and, believe me sweetie, I didn't like the evil red
eyes he'd got set into his flat little head. They were going up and down my
body like I was Miss Anthropoid of 1980. I heard Marlin Perkins's voice in

24

my head again: "These harmless cousins of ours are curious by nature, and
will rape and pillage anything in their path."

Well, I stood still until that goddamn ape slowly reached out a hand, just
like in 2001, and almost grabbed my boob.

Nobody grabs my boob. That's when I went for the sword. *Whip.* I was
standing straight and fierce and beautiful, ready to defend my honor if I
had to skewer all twenty of them. The ape gives me this beady stare. Then
it goes *ptui* and spits out the dead animal. "What are you doing in Yag-
Nash's territory?" he goes. In pretty good English, yet (with just a trace of a
regional accent, but let's not get snobby). I'd been astonished to find that
people on Mars spoke English. Now these apes or ape-men or whatever
they were did the same thing. Don't ask me to explain it: I'm just a fighting
woman.

I go, "Nothing. I come in peace." I took it that this was Yag-Nash himself
I was dealing with.

Another of these talking Neandertals came up and looked me over, the
same as Yag-Nash had, and goes, "Let's kill the she now. The feathered
snake will not feed the whole tribe." It kicked the scruffy dead thing on the
ground.

"No," goes Yag-Nash, "the she will not die. The tribe of Yag-Nash has
had bad hunting since the death of the High Priestess. This beautiful she
will be our new High Priestess." All the other ugly, hairy brutes opened
their eyes wide and started going, "Ohhhhh."

"Thank you for saving my life," I go.

"Don't mention it," goes Yag-Nash. They were real Missing Links, Bitsy.
I wish they'd stayed Missing.

I breathed a little easier, but I didn't lower my sword. Something I
learned on Mars: don't trust anybody except handsome princes; *especially*
don't trust horribly blechy things from *The Twilight Zone.* I didn't like
being all pink and perky and undressed in front of these hairballs, but I
couldn't get my clothes on and keep them covered at the same time. My
problem was solved for me by ol' Yag-Nash, the leader of the pack.

"Bring her along to the caves," he goes. And the twenty of them
swarmed all over me, and grabbed my arms and legs and lifted me off the
ground. I hung on to Old Betsy, but she didn't do me any good, you know?
I didn't have a chance to get in a good whack at any of them. They kept up
this weirdo moaning chant as they carried me through the jungle. I twisted
my head a little, and I saw that none of them had thought to bring along my

suitcase. Good-bye new outfits; good-bye *Je Reviens*. And after all that hard shopping we did, too. I never *did* get to wear any of that stuff.

When we got to their place—it was like this cliff with caves poked into it like the little holes in a slice of rye bread—they carried me up to the main cave. I don't know how they climbed that cliff. It sure looked sheer and smooth to me. But then, I don't have arms that swing below my knees, or fighting fangs either. We human beings have lost a little something to make up for what we've gained on our Long March Toward Civilization. Thank the Lord.

When they deposited me on the floor of the main cave—*ba-WHUMP*— Yag-Nash gestured and the rest of them left in a hurry. He looked down at me with those cruddy little beady eyes of his. He drooled, Bitsy, he really *drooled.* Like my Uncle Jerry.

I go, "You didn't bring my clothes along. You have anything here for me to wear?"

His expression went blank for a second, then he must have had what passed for an idea in his little pea-brain. "I will garb you with the richness and finery of last High Priestess," he goes. "You will like Yag-Nash then. You will be *grateful.*"

"You bet," I go. I shuddered a little.

The boss ape hustled out on his short, bowed legs. I had a few minutes to myself, but so what? The main cave was huge, but it didn't lead anywhere and I couldn't climb down that cliff by myself. I was trapped there. I clutched Old Betsy and waited. A little while later my pal came back, carrying a double armload of stuff. He dropped it at my feet. "What's that?" I go.

"Wear," he goes instructively.

I sorted through the stuff. At first it looked like a hopeless mess of tangled braids and straps. I couldn't make heads or tails out of it. I carried it all to the light at the mouth of the cave and I gasped, like, Bitsy, it was all *gold* and *jewels!* I mean, *all* of it! There was this bra kind of thing with dangling golden loops and chains and thingies hooked up front to back and all, and a sexy little G-string of gold with a thin little gold hipband. Wow, if I'd have had that stuff on some football weekend up in New Haven . . . ! And the gold was just lousy with jewels. *Covered* with jewels, all emeralds, some as big as a quarter. "This is for *me?*" I go.

"Wear," Yag-Nash goes. He was the strong, silent type.

I put it on. Well, gold is nice to look at and appraise and all, but it's not much fun to live in. The bra wasn't lined or anything, and the metal edges dug into my skin. The girl who had it before me must have been two full cup-sizes smaller, 'cause my boobs were all squashed together and hauled up almost to my shoulders. Did *terrific* things for my cleavage, but it was uncomfortable as all hell. And the metal G-string was *cold*. Yipe.

"Good," goes Yag-Nash, when I had, uh, garbed myself.

"Glad you like it," I go. *"Now* what?"

"We hunt again tomorrow. Before the hunt, you must pray to the Great Rock-Sky God!"

"Sure," I go. I knew that was breaking some commandment or something, but desperate times call for desperate measures.

"Now you sleep."

I go, "But I'm not tired. I'll wait until tonight."

"What do you mean, 'night'?"

Then I realized, like, it wasn't *ever* going to get dark. The little sun in the middle of the Earth never set. So much for sneaking away after the sun went down, as if there were anywhere to sneak *to*. I stretched out on the cave floor—it was just crawling with bugs and spiders, of course—and after a while, I don't know how long, I went to sleep.

I had a surprise when I woke up. Yag-Nash had shackled my right ankle and chained me to the wall. "Great," I thought, "that's all I need." Like it made any difference, though before, at least I had the *illusion* of freedom. I still had my sword. The only thing I could figure out was that Yag-Nash didn't recognize Old Betsy as a weapon. He may never have seen a sword before. I hoped I could make him more familiar with it Real Soon Now.

Hours later, I suppose, Yag-Nash came back into the cave huffing and puffing from the climb up the rock face. "It is time, O High Priestess," he goes.

"Well," I thought, *"every* High Priestess has to start sometime." Yag-Nash held something in his hand. His attitude was different now: he was respectful, almost timid. I looked at what he was offering me—it was a big golden crown set with emeralds and huge diamonds. I could have bought Massachusetts, furnished, with that, for God's sake. I took it and plopped it on my head. Then Yag-Nash threw me over his shoulder without a word, not so much as an "Excuse me, Exalted One," and started down the cliff. I shut my eyes and practiced praying.

There was a sort of flat altar made of roughly shaped rock about a hundred yards into the jungle. The rest of the tribe—I guess there were about a hundred in all—was spread through the big clearing, and they were all chanting and grunting and jumping up and down on their knuckles. It was

disgusting. Yag-Nash walked into the middle of the clearing, by this altar
thing, and raised his furry arms. "Silence!" he goes.

There was silence.

Then it was *my* turn. I went up to the altar and looked around at my
congregation. I put a stern look on my face—see, I figured from Yag-Nash's
attitude that as High Priestess I was some big hoo-ha now, and I wanted to
see how far I could push it. "First off," I go in a kind of cop voice, loud and
commanding, "I don't want you to call me High Priestess. 'Priestess' is a
sexist label. I won't have any of that. You will call me Reverend Maureen."

The Neandertals nodded their huge, lumpy heads. "Mo-reen," they murmured.

"That's fine. Now as I understand it, you're about to go on another hunt
today. I will say a prayer for your success. I will invoke the blessing of the
Great Rock-Sky God on you. I will bring meat for your hungry, hairy
bellies. You will treat me with deference."

"Mo-reen," they all go.

"Damn right." Then I went into the prayers, something like, "Heavenly
Father, we are gathered here together to ask your blessing on our hunters.
Today they go out in search of food for their shes and young ones. Game is
scarce, and the animals are cunning or fleet of foot. Our hunters are neither, and they are armed only with these cruddy stone knives that couldn't
stab their way through wet newspaper. What's more, our hunters don't
have the largest cranial capacities, if you know what I mean—and *they
don't,* or I'd be in trouble now. Therefore, we ask that you make it easy on
them. A few deer or something trapped in a tar pit would be nice. I don't
expect miracles, but like, *I* get hungry, too, right? I guess that's about all.
Thanking you in advance, this is Reverend Maureen, signing off."

"Amen," murmured the cavemen.

Yag-Nash goes, "You pray good, Mo-reen. You are a good High—I mean,
a good Reverend."

I shrugged. "It's a gift," I go. "I will bring you much meat. I will end
hunger and want among the tribe of Yag-Nash."

"Good," he goes.

"And you will treat me well."

The pot-bellied old creep gave me that slimy squint again. "You will like
the way Yag-Nash treats you," he goes. I doubted that very seriously. He
grabbed me and carted me out of the clearing, back to the main cave and
the shackle and chain. I complained, but it didn't do any good. And he took
the crown, too. *That's* the kind of man I attract, Bitsy, ain't it the truth? He

left me in the cave all alone, secured to the wall. From far away I could hear the shouts of the hunters as they worked themselves up into a sweat.

Well, this kind of thing went on for one hell of a long time. They'd feed me and bring me water, but that was all. No washing, no exercise, *nothing*. I was wasting away. Every couple of "days" Yag-Nash would carry in the crown and trundle me down the cliff to the altar, where I said a prayer and everybody acted subdued and courteous for a few minutes. Then it was back to the cave and the chain and Maureen Birnbaum, Prisoner of Love. The funny thing was, the hunters *did* have better luck. They came back with lots of meat, or else I suppose they'd have killed—and maybe eaten— me. I figure that's what happened to the last High Priestess. Yucko. The hunters brought back these big old reindeer and musk oxen and things. I mean, animals you don't find walking around the woods on the surface anymore. The reindeer and oxen were *gigantic*. They were prehistoric animals, just like Yag-Nash and his crew. I knew that for sure when they brought in the wooly mammoth. You could tell it wasn't just a plain old elephant: it was a *mammoth*. And they killed other weird critters, too: saber-toothed tigers and beavers the size of bears and sloths as big as hippos. But my congregation had a lot to learn about the fine points of the culinary arts: *Cuisine Primitif,* you know, the Food of the Clods. Fire-blackened here and there on the outside, bloody raw on the inside. I was hungry all the time, so I got to where I liked it that way.

After this went on for many months—I filled up the wall as far as I could reach with "daily" scratches—Yag-Nash came into the cave in a real dither. I'd kept him away from me by telling him that if he put one paw on my reverend bod, the Great Rock-Sky God would punish him by driving away all the game. Yag-Nash was hungry more often than he was horny, so I didn't have to worry about him except when his dim bulb of a brain forgot my threat. When he came in all excited, I figured, "Here we go again."

I was wrong. He goes, "We have captured an enemy."

This was some news. I mean, I didn't even *know* there was another tribe anywhere nearby. "Uh-huh," I go.

"It is a morthak, not like Yag-Nash and his people. You must sacrifice it to the Great Rock-Sky God."

"Sacrifice?" Bitsy, I can't even bring myself to squish a goddamn *cockroach*. On Mars I lopped some heads off these big green men, but that was purely self-defense. Cutting out hearts on an altar is something else. I didn't know what a morthak was, but whatever it was, I didn't think I could kill it.

29

"The morthak must die," Yag-Nash goes, "or *you* will take its place."

Well, on second thought, maybe this prehistoric world *could* get along without a crummy morthak one way or the other.

Yag-Nash gave me the glitzy crown and I put it on, then he unlocked me and tossed me over his shoulder and we made our way down the cliff. I'd gotten pretty used to it by now, you know? I didn't have to close my eyes anymore. I even kept up a pleasant stream of chatter. I mean, I didn't have all that many "people" to talk to. Not that Yag-Nash was the most scintillating conversationalist. His idea of a snappy comeback was "Gruh!"

I had another surprise waiting for me when we got to my altar. A "morthak" turned out to be a good-looking boy with a fearless smile to *die* for. I *mean* it, Bitsy. This guy made Prince Van look like Ernest Borgnine or something. He wasn't blond and he didn't have blue eyes, but you can't have *everything*. He was wearing this navy blue jumpsuit, so I knew he probably came from up on the surface too. In all the time I'd been in the center of the Earth, I hadn't seen anybody else like me. A *person*, you know? So I stood beside the altar where they had this gorgeous specimen tied down, and I go, "Where did you go to school?"

He looked at me all surprised. "Nathanael West High School in New York," he goes.

I was a little disappointed. I go, "Oh, like a *public school* kid." Well, *everybody* can't go to Andover or Exeter or Lawrenceville. I mean, there are probably rich and powerful corporation executives who started out in some public school system and showed a lot of potential and made their way on smarts and ambition. But, see, I wasn't interested in a guy with just *promise*. I was looking for somebody who had more to fall back on than a cute little tush.

"You know the world I come from?" he goes.

I had to laugh. "*I* come from the world you come from," I go. "If I was still there and hadn't had all these adventures and everything, I'd be a senior at the Greenberg School."

He goes, "I have a sort of friend whose sister goes to the Greenberg School."

"Oh, really?" I go. "What's her name?"

"Jennifer Freeman. She's a sophomore."

"Oh, well," I go, drawing myself up kind of haughtily, "we don't hang out with *sophomores*."

"My name is Rod Marquand," he goes. "I'm pleased to meet you."

"I'm—"

30

I was rudely interrupted by Yag-Nash. He pushed a golden knife in my hands and growled, "Kill him."

"What?" I go. *"Him?"*

"Kill."

"Hey, look. I thought he was going to be this *morthak* or something. I can't kill a live human being."

"Kill him or die yourself."

This Rod guy goes, "Go ahead, then, young lady. If *that's* the situation, please, save yourself. I'll die happily, knowing that you're safe." What a sweet, brave boy. If only he didn't go to public school.

"I can't do that," I go.

Yag-Nash was furious. "Take them both back to the cave!" And the tribe grabbed us and hauled us up to the main cave. I was shackled and Rod was tied up hand and foot. Just before he left, Yag-Nash turned to me and goes, "You'll die a horrible death, Mo-reen. You will fill the belly of Yag-Nash!" And he laughed, sort of. It was *awful*.

When we were alone, Rod looked at me and smiled. "Thanks for not killing me," he goes.

"You're very welcome, I'm sure. Look where it got me."

"Don't be alarmed, Miss. I'll get us out of here. I came here in an atomic subterrine. We'll escape in that."

"What is it?" I go. It sounded like a tiny soup bowl that ran on atomic power.

"It's a submarine that moves through solid rock instead of water. I built it myself. I'm a kind of inventor," he goes.

"Great, but we're stuck up here a million feet off the goddamn ground."

"Don't worry about that, either. When I'm not inventing or going to school, I also fight crime in the guise of a costumed superhero. I can't tell you my secret identity. I'm sorry."

"That's okay," I go. I mean, Bitsy, this kid had *promise* the way most guys have obnoxious *ideas*, if you get what I mean.

"Close your eyes," he goes. I did. I heard this popping sound, and when I opened my eyes again, his ropes were lying on the floor of the cave and he was *gone*.

A little while later I heard this humming noise, and a periscope poked up through the floor about twenty feet away. It turned around a little and pointed at me for a second. Then the top part of the submar—I mean, subterrine—surfaced. Rod opened the hatch and climbed out. "How do you like her?" he goes. He was real proud of it, you could tell.

"She's terrific—get me the hell *out* of here!"

"Sure." He came over and snapped my shackle like it was a stolen credit card.

"I'd kind of like to take my crown with me," I go. I really didn't want to go without it. I mean, I have my old age to plan for.

"We can't take the chance. We'll have to leave it behind." Why is it that heroes are so goddamn *practical?* I just *knew* he was going to say that. Anyway, there was enough gold and emeralds in what I was wearing to support me for a while. I shrugged. I can be realistic when I want. So he helped me up the ladder and into this cramped ship of his. He closed the hatch and started punching buttons and turning wheels. There was an incredible rocking motion like the A train between Fifty-ninth Street and 125th Street. I thought I was going to *tossez mes doughnuts* right there or something. "We're making good speed," Rod goes.

"Wonderful." I felt sick as the proverbial dog.

Well, Bitsy, it was a rough ride home. There weren't any windows because there was only rock going by. I mean, I *suppose* Rod's invention was brilliant and amazing and all, but it will be a long time before the guy books *cruises* or anything. The Love Boat it ain't—in more ways than one. I'll have to tell you *all* about this Rod Marquand sometime. He was dedicated, Bitsy. I mean *dedicated.* To science and fighting crime. He figured we were almost home, see, and I go, "Why don't we have lunch or something?" He turned me *down,* sweeties, do you believe *that?* His uncle, the physicist, would be waiting for a report, and besides, there was a whole rash of unsolved crimes recently in New York, and he owed it to his parents to hurry right home, and by then I told him to just *forget* it.

"Where are we now?"

"We're just passing through the lowest level of Penn Station," he goes.

"You can let me out here," I go. I was in a *huff*. Look, not even this boy genius can turn down Mo-reen, She-God of the Muck People.

"But—"

"*Let me out!*" I go, kind of brandishing Old Betsy. I was frustrated that I never did get my licks in against Yag-Nash, and I was just *dying* to start a fight.

Rod stopped the machine and opened the hatch. I squeezed on by him and went up the ladder and looked around. We were now on the second level, not far from the escalator that takes you up to Thirty-Fourth Street. I looked down at Rod and I go, "You better sail on out of here, honey, people are gawking." Then I climbed down the outside of the ladder. The hatch

32

clanged behind me, and the subterrine dived into the floor. I walked toward the escalator, swishing my sword in little angry circles. People got out of my way, *fast.*

I had to walk to the diamond district, but it wasn't that far. You should have seen the looks I got from the old guys in the place I went into! I mean, wearing this golden bra and G-string and slashing around with Old Betsy and all. I wonder what I looked like to them. I pried a little emerald out of my raiment and sold it. They gave me a big song and dance about how illegal it all was, but I could see they wanted to get their greedy hands on the emerald and all the rest of it. They offered me a hundred bucks—like I was from out of town, right? I laughed. It was like dickering with Pammy, my stepmother. I ended up getting my price for it, but only by promising that I wouldn't let anyone else buy any of the other jewels. The emeralds are rare and perfect or something. I was going to pay you back the money I owed you out of that cash—see, I *didn't* forget—but when you went on your vacation instead of seeing me, I figured, "The hell with *her.*" Instead, you'll find a nice-size emerald on your coffee table, and let you go through all the red tape trying to explain where you got it and everything. If you ever do, pay your mother back for me.

The tape's about finished, Bitsy. I'll see you when you get back from your trip. I hope you're sunburned as hell.

WELL, SHE WASN'T THERE *when I got back. There were only the tape cassette, the emerald, and one god-awful mess in the kitchen. You'd have thought the Marines had camped out there on their way to the Halls of Montezuma or something. I can't imagine why Muffy—I mean, Maureen—didn't wait for me. She must have this itch for adventure now, I guess, and went whooshing off to some new aggravation somewhere, sometime.*

Speaking of aggravation, I got more than she bargained for with that goddamn emerald. I mean, I almost did time in jail on account of it. I'm still not square with the IRS or anybody. I really want to talk to Maureen about that, believe me. Sword or no sword, she's going to walk out of here with at least a bloody nose.

With any kind of luck, I'll hear from her soon. It will be worth having to sit through her whole stupid recitation to paste her one in the face. I can't wait.

33

Robert Adams, author of the popular *Horseclans* series, was a good friend and a fan of Muffy's adventures. He reprinted the two Burroughs pastiches in anthologies he edited. He also asked me to write a parody of the *Horseclans* novels for a third anthology, *Friends of the Horseclans.* I asked him if he really wanted me to mock his self-made universe, and he said that he couldn't wait to see what I came up with. So I said I'd be glad to give it a try. I took careful notes on several of his books, noting characters, history, geography, vocabulary, and so forth. The result follows.

P.S.: Bob liked it a lot

Maureen Birnbaum
on the Art of War

Maureen Birnbaum
on the Art of War

by Betsy Spiegelman

(as told to George Alec Effinger)

I HAD NEVER BEEN so deliriously, deliciously giddy in my life. I had only been married for three hours, and already everything was like happening exactly as I had hoped and dreamed since childhood. My whole family and all my friends agreed that Josh was a real catch. He was an M.D., a newly-graduated family practitioner. As a wedding present, his Uncle Mort Fein announced that he was retiring and like turning his long-established Queens practice over to my husband. My legs turned weak for yet another time; Uncle Mort's patients were all well-to-do and terribly loyal, and the gift also saved Josh and me a considerable amount of money that we assumed we'd have to borrow to get Josh's office set up, not to mention the long years it would otherwise have taken to develop a good practice from scratch. It was as if Uncle Mort had, with one stroke, like fully insured our futures. On top of that, Mums shook loose a considerable sum from her "holdings," as she called them. All the rest of the family and Josh's family followed suit. I felt a little guilty about being exhilarated by all those dollar signs, but Josh said it was perfectly normal to be dazzled by such a windfall. He said that he was, too.

Right after the reception we caught a plane to our honeymoon vacation in

37

Bermuda. Josh's younger sister is like a travel agent; she made all the arrangements and used her pull to get us a terrific discount, even though it was the height of the season. I don't have a single memory of the flight itself. We flew first class, of course; and as soon as the flight attendants learned we were newlyweds, they started hitting us with champagne, even before the plane pulled away from the terminal building. The bubbly wine and the pressure in the cabin combined to relax me so much that my next conscious memory is of Josh holding me in his arms and trying to unlock the door to our honeymoon suite. Like I don't even recall checking in, you know? "Josh, honey," I go, showing my down-to-earth, level-headed side right at the beginning of our new partnership, "put me down, unlock the door, open it, and then, like, pick me up again."

"You're brilliant and beautiful, Betsy." Josh can never bring himself to use my old high school and college nickname.

I kissed him. Then, after he'd opened the door and carried me across the threshold, he put me gently down on the gigantic bed. He gave me a comic leer and I giggled. Then we looked at each other. Neither of us could think of anything to say or do. Like, what came next?

"Well," goes my darling, "how does it feel to be Mrs. Dr. Josh Fein, King of Queens with eyes cast rapaciously toward Manhattan?"

"Cast your eyes rapaciously toward me and nobody or nothing else," I go. I took a few deep breaths and let myself calm down. That's when I noticed how absolutely beautiful our suite was, and the view through the picture windows of the gardens and the sea beyond. "Josh," I go, "let me go into the bathroom and put on something more romantic. I packed some special things and I've like planned this moment ever since eighth grade."

He smiled at me. "All right," he goes. "I'll open the champagne and turn down the bed." He wiggled his eyebrows at me suggestively. I giggled again. Josh just cracks me up.

I grabbed one of my suitcases and went into the bathroom. I had a little trouble with my dress, and I struggled with it for a moment. Then I heard a voice go, "You need some help with that?" It hadn't been Josh's voice. I whirled around.

Damn it all to hell if it wasn't Muffy—I mean, Maureen—Birnbaum. I could see by her outfit that she'd just come back from one of her nauseating exploits. I remembered the promise I'd made myself, when she'd left a huge emerald to reimburse me for an old debt. She thought she was playing a joke on me with that gem, but it got me into no end of trouble. I declared that the next time I saw the girl, I was like going to break her face for her.

Well, I didn't. Instead, I went straight for her pure and innocent eyes. Maureen reacted more quickly than you'd think such a full-figured girl could. Her fist came up in this long, clean arc and detonated on the point of my chin. I thought I heard a little grinding of bone. The world went black and I was falling over backward, watching bright red points of light glimmering like fireflies in the gloom. I heard Maureen from a long distance away. "Bitsy, hell, Bitsy! Oh, wow, I didn't mean to hit you. Not so hard, I mean. I got you, you'll be all right. You'll have maybe just a bad bruise, that's all. Come on. Like, shake it off!" She threw cold water on me, for which I could have killed her. I found that I was sitting on the edge of the bathtub. Maureen was regarding me anxiously from her perch on the beige chenille-covered toilet lid.

"Goddamn, Muffy," I go, gingerly feeling my jaw, "I'm on my honeymoon, and now I'll probably have to like take all my meals through a straw." I couldn't imagine how we ever could have been friends.

"It'll be worth it, to hear the story I've got this time," she goes. I really wanted to hand her head to her, but I was still stunned.

"You die, bitch," was all I could hoarsely murmur.

"Calm down, Bitsy," she goes. "You want to like change outfits? Get out of that geeky schmatte and I'll find your little bit of nothing in here."

I did as she said, wobbling my jaw every now and then, feeling my head pound and throb as I wriggled out of my $380 Neiman-Marcus "schmatte."

"This is like what you wanted?" goes Maureen, extending the drop-dead lavender gauzy chemise and panty set. "Victoria's Secret? I don't know them, but I do know their secret: they know you don't have any like boobs."

My right hand clenched slowly into a hard fist.

Maureen just laughed. "Hey, ease up, Bitsy. You always zinged me about my fat ass, I always zinged you about being titless."

"Yeah," I muttered. That's when I first really noticed what she was wearing: leather pants tucked into high boots, very butch; a sleeveless quilted cotton shirt covered with chain mail, I mean, for God's sake; and some kind of crested helmet pushed back on her head. She wore her old sword—the one she'd picked up on Mars—on one hip. On the other hip she had a new sword, bigger, and like a dagger. She had a spear and a large sack of some rough, filthy material. She looked like a combination of Santa Claus and Joan of Arc. Can you believe it? Sometimes I doubt she really has these adventures. I think she like goes away for a year or more and makes up some ridiculous Mardi Gras outfit and comes back just to see how much she can

annoy me. She's either a for-sure scientific enigma or she's really like psy-cho, you know? "For Christ's sake, Muffy, where *have you been?*"

She grinned at me. She never grinned before; she'd smile or she'd laugh, but she never grinned. She was losing that fine edge the Greenberg School had labored so long and so futilely to apply to her. "Run the shower so Mr. Honeybunch doesn't wonder what's going on in here."

I reached behind myself and turned on the taps full blast.

"Good," she goes. "Now, wait until you hear this story. And if you call me Muffy again, I'll brain you."

IWAS READY, *believe* me, I was *more* than ready to hang up my sword; but, like, two things occurred to me. The first was that there wouldn't be anybody to look out for the wretched and downtrodden on all these planets without me, and the second was that every time I have an adventure I meet a real cute boy. That was better odds than I used to get at the Greenberg School. So I didn't retire Ol' Betsy after all. I decided to go for one last shot at finding Mars and Prince Van. I mean, like, it wasn't *his* fault that I got lost, was it? Let's be fair about this, now.

I put together another full-on collection of wearables, crammed into two Oh-They're-Just-Something-I-Stumbled-Over bags that leaped at my throat from a page in the Bean catalog. I decided on the college sophomore look. You know: too old to be a *total* squid, but young enough so that the Manda-tory Party Rule is still in effect. I had on a beige shirtdress with blue pins, a 'shmere sweater tied around my neck, and a pair of raggedy old Pumas on my feet. Come nightfall, I looked into the sky and felt a tug toward the God of War. I barely had to whoosh myself; like it was almost whooshed for me. The going was getting easier every time I tried it.

But goddamn it, the steering was as slippery as it ever was. Right from the second when I blammed into a big old tree, I knew I'd missed Mars again. And Mars is like a *big place*, right? You'd think it'd be easy enough to hit. Well, let's see *you* try it. Get back to me on that.

Anyway, where I did end up, I was smushed against this tree. I couldn't tell you what *kind* of tree, except it had bark—it had bark in my mouth, jammed into my nose, cutting up my knees. I was thinking, "Maureen Birnbaum killed by tree. Details on the hour." The tree was like making no move to back off, so *I* did. I looked around and there were no witnesses, so I didn't feel like such a total wheeze.

There was a dusty dirt road behind me, winding through all the trees. I didn't know which way I ought to go, so I thought I'd just kind of sit down with my Bean bags and wait for someone to come along. So it figures, as soon as I sit down, my *imagination* starts to work—maybe I'm all alone on this planet with like a road.

Chill out, *Maureen.* In a few minutes I hear a lot of clanking and bumping and rattling. Traffic sounds. Not I-95 traffic sounds, you know, but at least *some* creatures were hustling their buns toward me. I asked myself, I go, "Maureen, is that necessarily like a good thing?" So I take my bags and my sword and hide out behind this clump of underbrush. A few minutes later I see this little parade. There's a bunch of Schwarzenegger-types wearing hacked-up outfits, riding these big old horses that looked like a cross between a Clydesdale and a Peterbilt tractor. The men were all carrying swords and battleaxes and stuff.

They are fighting men. I have no problem with that. I got out from under the underbrush. "Hey," I go.

Three of these totally bluff guys leap on me—from their *horses*—and bring me up in front of their leader. They yammer at me in some language, it could have been Greek for all I knew.

Finally the leader, who's still up on his horse so I have to lean way back just to see his face—which was a *cute* face, in a sort of fierce and determined way, mature and all—this man leans down and gives me one of those amused little smiles. He goes, "May I ask your name, miss?"

I go, "You can call me Maureen, but I've bailed out of all those sexist mister-and-miss things."

He nodded pleasantly, but one of his young friends mutters something that sounded like "brahbehrnuh." Now, my *God,* Bitsy, you know I'm the last person in the *world* that would burn a bra. Without good underwired support, a fighting woman is just plain asking for trouble. Halfway through the action she'd be nearly *helpless,* what with the harmonic motion of her boobs interfering with her swordplay. I spun around real fast to see who'd made that little remark, but they looked at me all wide-eyed and innocent. Their leader goes, "Forgive them, they haven't met many twentieth-century women, and those they *have* met were without exception hostile."

"A typical generalization," I go. This is where I got all haughty. In the back of my mind, though, certain questions are just like *crying out* to be asked. "Where the hell *am* I?" seemed like a good start.

This man with the dark skin and the bright eyes goes, "You're a trifle

41

north of the Kingdom of New Kuhmbuhluhn, east on the road from the
ducal seat of Tchaimbuhsburk."

"I meant what *planet* is this?" I go.

He shrugged. "Earth," he goes. "What did you expect?"

"Earth? Then something's wrong."

"What year do you think it is?"

I'm like easy to get along with, so I told him. He says it was now more
than eight hundred years since civilization had been destroyed in a nuclear
holocaust. I looked at his weapons and his men's armor and the whole
knobby barbarian influence on this band of merry men. I didn't have any
trouble believing him. I mean, it couldn't be that they were only making,
you know, a daring fashion statement or something. Instead of traveling
through *space*, I'd traveled through *time*. Prince Van and you, Bitsy, and my
allowance were many hundreds of years in the past, dead and buried. I
paused a moment for emotion.

"My name is Milo," goes the leader. He saw that I was sort of like all
aufgeshaken, you know? He looked down from his horse and shook his
head, evidently deciding what he was going to do with me.

"You don't have to do *anything* with me," I go. "I can take care of
myself."

Milo nodded. "I was just curious about how you got here."

"I don't know."

"Well, you've walked into the middle of a war. We have to keep moving,
I plan to catch up with my army in the next few days. Maybe I'd better
detail one of my men to take you to a safe—"

"Hold on, Milo, old buddy," I go. I've never met anyone else named
Milo. The only Milo I'd ever even heard of was the Venus de. "I don't need
you to look out for me. You don't have to send one of your men—if that's,
you know, the right *word* for them—to escort me anywhere."

"You appear to be very independent, Miss Birnbaum." He gave me another smile.

I went immediately from merely haughty to fully stoked. "Get off that
goddamn *elephant!*" I yelled at him. I was stalking back to the bush to get
Ol' Betsy. We were going to see about this right now. I was so mad I didn't
even like ask myself how he knew my last name.

I'm waving my trusty blade in his face and the three soldiers are just
laughing their filthy, scungy heads off. Milo raised a hand and they
stopped. He held a locked case in his other hand. "I haven't used one of
these in centuries," he goes, taking a beautiful, gleaming saber from the

case. Its baskethilt's not jewel encrusted like mine, but I can see it's a nifty piece of work. "Toledo," he goes. "That wouldn't mean anything to the troopers of my Confederation, but perhaps you'll appreciate it."

"Appreciate *this*," I go. I salute him, spend a twelfth of a second *en garde*, and then lunge, apparently for his chest. I really meant to cut his wrist on the inside, but he saw that coming. He parried Quarte, with his blade nearly vertical, and merely tilted his forearm from the elbow, knocking my blade aside. His riposte came so damn fast that he almost got me. Milo shot his fist straight toward my chest, making a quick, short slash. I was forced to parry Quinte, which God only knows I'm not *good* at. My sword hand was high, near eye-level. I caught his attack okay, turned my wrist over, and lunged at him. The two of us went back and forth like that for a few minutes. I knew right off that like maybe I'd made a mistake. This guy was no Martian monster, for sure, and I didn't have low gravity on my side. Milo could have diced me up any time he wanted. I'm just real, real glad he didn't *want* to. Really.

Still, I was holding my own, you know, if only just barely. I could pick up on a murmured conversation behind me, the three hairball soldiers making comments. I like to think they were sort of astonished by how well I was handling their commanding officer. I hoped they couldn't see that Milo was carrying me.

That is, like he carried me for a while until I made a dumb goof. He feinted at my wrist, then bent his elbow and brought his point up and cut at my left shoulder. I wasn't sure what to do, and I parried wrong. Before I could attack, he scored with a remise, putting his saber completely through my shoulder just above the armpit. "*Goddamn it!*" I yelled. "*Goddamn son of a bitch!*" I was hopping around in pain and swearing like a, well, trooper. I dropped Ol' Betsy and clutched my shoulder. A little blood spurted out and stained my brand new shirtdress. I hadn't worn it more than a couple of hours. Milo was really sorry. He put his sword down and hurried to me.

"Are you all right?" he goes.

I just glared at him. "It hurts like homemade *hell*," I go.

"Let me see," he goes.

"Are you *kidding* me? Here, just take all my clothes off and examine my booboo. Fat chance, buster."

"I'm just—"

"I know, I know. It's all my fault, I'm just being unreasonable, I asked for it. That's what Daddy tells me all the time. *Ouch.*"

His eyes narrowed a bit. "Take your hand away, at least."

I did. The wound had stopped bleeding already.

Milo gave me a long, thoughtful look. "Lift up the material and tell me what you see."

I did. "It's *healed!*" I go. I was amazed, if you want to know the truth.

Milo rubbed his jaw with one hand. "I'd be grateful if you'd travel with me for a few days," he goes. "I'd like to talk with you about a few matters that are important to this world."

That was better. It showed he was a gentleman and not just some kind of gross, chauvinist Captain Future. "Will I get to see some of your war?" I go.

"You won't be able to avoid it."

"Neat. Let me get my things." One of the soldiers helped stow my two bags on his huge horse. Milo lifted me up to his saddle, and I clung to him as we rode. His beautiful chestnut stallion was so big, I couldn't get my legs around it. I felt like I was doing splits on a gym floor, for Christ's sake.

Milo talked as we traveled. Apparently, some upstart had formed a pocket kingdom he called Kehnooryees Ahkeeyuh, or New Achaea. This bozo, who crowned himself King Pahleebohaitees I, worked for a while making allies and raising an army. He merged the city of Ritchmuhnd and several nearby villages, and called the result his capital, Kehnooryees Spahrtuh. His Union of Pure-Blooded Ehleenee let the Undying High Lord Milo know that it was dropping out of his Confederation. Not only that, but like it was making a beasty *pain* of itself by raiding the prosperous lands to the north and west. It was all the combined forces of the Confederation, the Kindred dragoons of the Middle Kingdoms, the Ahrmehnee troops, and the Moon Maiden archers could do to contain the rebellion. It still wasn't clear if they could defeat it. Milo expected me to know what the hell he was talking about, but like I was lost from Word One, I'm sure.

A few hours later we whammed into the tail-end of his army. The soldiers all cheered for Milo like he was Napoleon or What's-His-Name MacArthur or something. I could definitely handle inspiring that kind of reaction, but all my adventures have been one-on-one, you know, and like this was my first for-real war. Milo wanted to know which side I was going to be on, his or this bogue King Pahleebohaitees' Union. I go, "I know who *you* are, what's this Union?"

"Just renegade Ehleenee," he goes.

That like decided it for me. "Illini?" I go, with a suitable avant-barf expression. "Oh my *God*, that's like the Big Ten! Pammy, my stepmother, you know, she gave me three harsh rules about finding a husband: One, marry Yale first; if you can't get Yale, marry Princeton; if you can't get Yale or Princeton, devote yourself to a life of public service, like Mother Teresa. I'll never have a house in Newport if I hang around with Illini ag-school jocks. *Urrr.*"

Milo just shook his head again. He said something in that other language to one of the soldiers, then he turned back to me. "Just go with Duhlainee, he'll take you to the armorer. You're very good with that saber, but it won't help you very much against the weapons you'll be seeing soon."

The armorer fixed me up with just what I wanted. I got a *crushin'* longsword, lighter than what Milo carried. I could barely lift one of the big suckers off the ground, but I could swing the smaller sword with both hands. I figured like I'd be a hell of a lot quicker on the draw than those big zods. One of the guys takes a hack with his sword, he needs five minutes to recover for another swipe. Meanwhile, I could shred him with a combo of point and edge work. I also took this tasty dirk and a spear. I wanted a helmet, too—an open-faced helmet with the nose piece like the ancient Greeks wore, okay? With the spear and the helmet I'd look just so *kill*, like Athena, who was fully ruff and a legend in her own time.

"Nose piece," the armorer goes, in this fractured language they called Mehrikan. I could barely make out what he was like saying. "You got a big nose on you to protect."

I just gave him my Number Eight Smile—icy, totally aggro, *Warning to Others: This is Dangerous Territory.* "You want to like do your job? I don't *need* your constructive criticism."

He shrugged. "What about your shield?"

I hadn't planned to carry one, I was going to use both hands on the sword, right? I told him, and his eyes got wider. He muttered something under his breath: "Ahnaiyeestah." I found out it meant "without a shield," and that's what that bunch called me from then on: Mahreenah Ahnaiyeestah. My *nom de guerre,* can you believe it?

I also got this way rad draped white gown that I could wear with my crested helmet and spear and like *really* do the Athena number; and I was fitted with *this* outfit, the leathers and the chain mail, for battle. I was all set. Now we were hauling ass all over the countryside looking for the Union army.

So a couple of days later, still moving east, we get a frantic report: like the advance guards of *Thoheeks* Djaik Morguhn's Red Eagle warriors made contact with these hungry Pure-Blood Union foragers. "I didn't want to fight a battle here," goes Milo. "And, I'll wager, neither did Senior *Strahteegos* Lahmbrohs, our shrewd enemy. But look at the map; it is a coincidence, nothing more, forced on us by geography. This town is the junction of all the main roads for many miles around. I hoped that we would pass through it well ahead of the Union troops. I wanted to put my army between Lahmbrohs and his source of supply, far away in Karaleenos. There's nothing to be gained by wishing it was otherwise. I'll reinforce Djaik Morguhn and hope that Lahmbrohs chooses to disengage. There are more favorable places to come to grips." Milo looks at Prince Bili, Djaik's older brother, and Bili nods. I didn't offer any advice, 'cause like I didn't have any. In Milo's tent, it all looked like toy soldiers on a gameboard, but it was really weird on account of I knew men had already started to die for real.

Milo sent out his orders. *Thoheeks* Djaik was to hurry to bail out his advance unit and do what he could to slow down the withdrawal of Lahmbrohs and his Union rebels. Meanwhile, the Confederate units, scattered all across the damn countryside, would zoom up as fast as their mammoth-horses could carry them.

I was like just hot to get into my first battle, you know, but everybody I talked to kept saying, "Just wait, you'll see." Nobody would tell me *what* I'd see, and I thought maybe they didn't want to fight. That was dumb. I should have known better. They were all brave dudes—*stark* was their word—and they'd tussle every time they had to. It was only like they could think of other things they'd rather be doing. I know about that: I was very popular on Saturday nights. I mean, it was that Athena look that did it. And it was the Athena look plus the spear and the longsword that kept them from bipping my boobs, too. See, you don't feel up a warrior-woman. Not if you don't want people calling you "Lefty" for the rest of your life, I'm sure.

In the middle of the next morning, Milo got another report from Djaik Morguhn—he had sent a third of his infantry and cavalry to the town, under *Strahteegos* Kehrtuhs Hwiltuhn. Hwiltuhn was ordered to see what the Union *Strahteegos* planned to do, and to like head back toward our main body when he got that news. Things sort of didn't work out the way Milo and Djaik planned. Hwiltuhn did as he was told, but like when he got to the town, the battle was already boiling and he couldn't fall back. A whole horde of Ehleenee hodads were riding into town from the other direction, but most of the Union troops were like still quite a ways away. Old Hwiltuhn was famous for staying in fights when other leaders might decide to retreat. His men loved him for his guts and his totally hot-blooded but battle-wise experience. Hwiltuhn sent word that whether Milo wanted it or not, the fighting was going to happen around this sleepy town.

He said he'd like try to slow the enemy up as much as possible while Milo got the rest of the Confederation Army to the front lines. He was busily sheltering his men in a thin forest across a bare field from the Ehleenee, when a few arrows from the Union *kahtahfrahktoee* fell around them. One skanky arrow caught old Hwiltuhn in the throat, and he fell right to the ground, like totally dead. No others of his men were wounded. The battle was like begun, okay?

Milo let out this long, deep breath when he heard the news. "Kehrt was a good man," he goes, "one of the best." He shook his head a couple of times, and like that was *it*. He couldn't spare more time grieving for his old friend, there was warlording to do.

I had my own horse now, a small mare I called Mr. Ed. You're totally not going to believe *why* I called her Mr. Ed. Because I could *talk* to her. No, Bitsy, she wasn't a talking horse; she was like a *telepathic* horse. I heard her voice in my head, and she heard me. It like freaked me out at first; but we made friends fast, and she told me she'd been in battle before and I wouldn't have to like worry about leading her around, she'd know what I wanted and the best way to get there. We still had to catch up with the forward troops in the town, so Mr. Ed and I had a while to just kind of gossip, you know? Like you and I used to do. Turns out Milo with his tubular silver-streaked black hair was already married. I would have bet a million dollars that he was, but I had these *hopes*, okay?

Later that afternoon we came up to the town. Kehrtuhs Hwiltuhn's men had tried to hold their positions, but like there were just too many Ehleenee slimeballs pouring down on them. The bad guys seemed to have an ocean of reinforcements. Sooner or later the Confederation had to like back off, and they retreated at last right through the town. Now like you remember my Daddy, don't you, sweetie? The original Great Social Undertaking, dressed up like a WASP to get insight into the Goyische Experience. When he was told to put down his pencil and turn in his answer booklet, though, he figures out he's really hep to this way rad life. He had become an honest-and-true Them, I'm sure, okay? Like he traded his Abraham & Straus credit card for one that says *Penney's*, you should forgive the language. He got rid of the sexy Giorgio Armani aftershave I gave him for his birthday and started using Old Spice, like a *grandfather*, for God's sake. And he joined *clubs*, said it was good for business. He turned into—and I totally lost my lunches for two weeks when I heard this—one of those freaky guys who run around in toy uniforms carrying toy weapons and recreating historically heavyweight battles nobody hardly remembers anymore. Little puffs of white smoke and like dudes valiantly clutching their chests and going, "Oooh, I'm dead," then they got to lie around on the wet grass 'til everybody else is either dead, too, or historically captured or accepting somebody else's sword or something. Daddy clutched his chest a lot, 'cause dudes with more seniority got to be the hotshot conquerors. That didn't bother him any. A few more years he'd be General Sherman or George Washington, but he'd have to die his way into the good roles.

I got to watch these crispo mishmoshes, over and over. I learned some history and got like sunburnt and rained on. That's how when Milo and me and his army rode up to reinforce Kehrtuhs Hwiltuhn's panicky men, I made an observation that saved the Confederacy a bunch of time. I sat on a hilltop with Old Man Morai and it hit me like a kablooie from Athena or even Zeus himself: I pointed to another hilltop. I go, "That's *Little Round Top!*"

Milo goes, "Excuse me?"

"Little Round Top. I used to trudge all over this land with my Daddy. I know this place. I've studied every square inch a million times. That's Little Round Top, this is Cemetery Ridge we're stuck on, that's—"

"That must be Seminary Ridge," Milo goes in a quiet voice that for him was wild and crazy excitement.

"And the town is—"

"Getzburk."

"Gettysburg."

"That's right," Milo goes.

"Nothing new under the sun," I go.

"The geography makes the armies come together in the same place, for the same reasons. It really isn't such a huge coincidence."

"We'll like ponder it all later," I go. "Right now we've got a battle to fight. We'll see how close to real life it plays out."

"Sister Mahreenah, this *is* real life," he goes.

"Depends," I go. He was going to have to prove it to me, step by step. Then I started having like doubts, you know? "Oh my *God!* And you're the Confederacy, and the Confederacy *lost* the Battle of Gettysburg." I was scared, because I'll be the first one to admit that I don't always win. In fact, I was so insecure in those days, I thought of myself as the Black Hole of Victory, where winning was sucked down and lost forever, and defeat got bigger and blacker all around me.

"I assure you," Milo goes with a gentle smile, "the fact that *we're* the Confederation fighting a *Union* army at Gettysburg *is* mere coincidence. If

I recall my ancient history correctly, it was Meade's Army of the Potomac that occupied this part of the battlefield, and Lee's Army of Northern Virginia that attacked from *Strahteegos* Lahmbrohs's position. The words Confederacy and Union have been switched around, that's all."

"I'll like believe all that when I see them try Pickett's Charge, I'm sure, you know?"

"I doubt that they will," Milo goes. "It was an act of desperation back then. The chances of it happening again are very slight."

Yeah, right. Gag me with a supernova, okay? I mean, that was one *hell* of a bloody fight, thousands and thousands of dudes shot to like *bits*. And from what I'd seen, okay?, our "futuristic" medical team was just as primitive and clumsy as during the Civil War. You know, like no Demerol and no anesthetic and amputations done in the *dirt* with a *hacksaw*. If Milo hadn't told me that I was immortal, right, and all my wounds would heal *immediately,* I would have been nervous. Being immortal kind of lets you relax. I just felt sad for like all the troops who *weren't* undying, you know? All I could do that night was go up and down the Confederate line going "Where are you from, soldier?" and "There, there, everything will work out *just* fine." I felt like a crud.

One of these broad-shouldered madmen comes up to El Supremo and goes, "God-Milo, will we be attacking on the morrow?"

Old God-Milo gives his handsome head a little shake and goes, "No, Sekstuhn, we have almost an impregnable defensive formation here. We'll make the Union *kath-ahrohee* come to us, if they want to."

Another thing, sweetie: it sure does make a warrior-woman's mind rest easy to hear she's like *impregnable.*

Anyway, when Sekstuhn took the news back to his buddies, I go, "God-Milo?"

Milo just shrugged with an embarrassed smile on his face. "What can I say?" he goes. "Being immortal impresses my men as godlike."

"There is no god but Milo, and Prince Bili is his prophet," I go. "Let's see you make a *tree*, I'm *so sure.*"

"Get some rest, Mahreenah."

So I go, "*Bag it*, Milo." But I did catch some Z's.

The next morning, before first light, the whole Confederate line was buzzing with activity. We all ate a light breakfast and drank plenty of water; there probably wouldn't be any time to like stop and *refresh* ourselves during the battle. We checked over our weapons and horses and waited.

After a while, right, we checked them again. We were all restless, you know, waiting for the Ehleenee to like get their act together.

If I'd known what I was going to witness—and be a part of—I might *totally* have bailed out of there before dawn. I still have nightmares, you know? There was only one word to describe the fighting: totally *B-L-O-O-D-B-A-T-H*. I mean, it was one thing to lop the heads off green Martians and great apes, 'cause they were just *storybook* things to me. I didn't even *believe* in them while I was like cutting them to shreds. But maiming and killing *people*, that was completely Mondo Bummer.

The Union army had this idea, see, that they could bust through our lines. They were overconfident and they were like such total *jels* that they kept bonking themselves on our strong points. They'd make a charge at the left end of the line, squirm their way almost to the top of Cemetery Ridge, and then realize too late that they were no way going to cut through King Gilbuht's Harzburkers. The Blue Bear guys would work the Union butts until the Ehleenee would all go screaming EEK! back down the ridge. Then they'd try the Zunburk boys in the middle of the line. Same thing, like *tell* me about it. All morning that went on, back and forth. I held back at the beginning, trying to get the rhythm of it. Then I saw that the spazzy Greeks were working up to another run at the left. I kicked up Mr. Ed and went charging down on them. I don't know what got into me. I just got carried away, so *beat* me. I was lucky that the folks from the Duchy of Vawn got all revved, too, and came hollering and thundering behind me. In a minute I could hear them chanting: "Mahreenah Ahnaiyeestah! Mahreenah Ahnaiyeestah!" Like I was totally Sergeant York or somebody, I'm sure.

We slammed into the Ehleenee in a peach orchard. I didn't have *time* to be nervous, it was all I could do to stay *alive*. The first Union geek who took a run at me, I caught his sword on mine and turned it to the inside. While he was struggling to wind it back up, I just jabbed the point of my long-sword through his throat. It was so easy I laughed. Felt like spearing a *marshmallow* on the end of a *stick* or something.

A big cheer went up. I was a *hero!* I thought, "Maureen honey, you've *done* your part. Why don't you just trot yourself back up the hill and take ten?" But Mr. Ed was sending me these *awful* bloodlusty images. She was just itching to tromple somebody, I'm totally sure. It was like if I wanted to go back, I'd have to do it on *foot*, because Mr. Ed was not about to leave the battle. So I stayed, too. Horse and rider are one, I'm telling you, and you can't just *leave* your four-legged friend in the middle of a battlefield— Bad Show, Just Not Done.

I stood in the stirrups and nearly decapitated another Ehleenee slimeball before he could even unlimber his swordarm. Another cheer went up. I turned to flash the boys a courageous smile. While my head was turned, *jeez,* two of the bad guys came at me and like I never even *saw* them. One huge brawny Vawn person behind me spurred up and took out the nearer of the Ehleenee. He had time to deflect the second Ehleenee's sword thrust, but he deflected it right *at* me. I felt this way gross pain, like I'd been slashed right where my neck meets my shoulder. Didn't break any bones, but it *hurt* like holy hell. I went through my screaming and swearing number again, and I got a worried message from Mr. Ed. The Vawn cutie who came to my rescue turned around and supported me in the saddle while I gnashed my teeth and acted like *wholly* unladylike.

But then the bleeding stopped, and even *wickeder:* the wound closed and the pain went away. I thought I heard shouting from the axe-and-blade boys *before;* you should have like heard them when I showed I was, you know, halfway immortal myself. "Mahreenah! Mahreenah!" I could have totally sold them anything from then on. But business called.

I led the *thoheeks* of Vawn's brigade into the midst of the Ehleenee; and finally, after I'd sort of accounted for a dozen or so of the mega-nerds, they decided to book it out of there. We let them go and turned to reform on the ridge. No time to rest, though, 'cause like *another* batch of Union zods were trying us to the north. I let Mr. Ed take me to the action. It seemed to me that this battle was like shaping up just the same as the Civil War battle. No biggie, the defensive lines were in the same places, for the same reasons, you know? Cemetery Hill and Cemetery Ridge were the logical places to make a stand. Well, I knew that sooner or later, the Union was going to try the right again, making a bid for Cemetery Hill and Culp's Hill. I just didn't know *when.* All this time the fighting must have been *Heat City* down at Devil's Den, and I warned Milo to send some boys down to fully case it around.

About now I see this old, old dude walking up the back of the ridge. I go, "Just what we need, I'm sure, a *spy.*" So I bounce over to him and I go, "My good man."

"This's the battle, ain't it?" he goes.

Total Dudley. "Yup," I go.

"I come here to help out."

Now, it is *slightly* obvious to me that Nathan Hale here is like *completely* ancient, seventy years old and gray and grizzled, with this dinged-up old sword over his shoulder. I thought it was sweet of him to offer, but a

warrior woman and leader like myself can't take the time to watch after
these like *sightseers*. I start to open my mouth to tell him, you know, that
we all appreciated his *guts* and all, *but*. . . .

He rushes past me, whips his sword in a circle over his dumb-bunny
bald head, and hacks down an Ehleenee son of a bitch who had almost
snuck up on me. I blinked at the geezer, you know, totally freaked, but I
didn't know what to say. He looked up at me. Finally I go, "Very good.
Carry on," like I was the rockin' steady Milo Morai-type, which I'm not
when I've almost been killed.

I didn't see much of Grandpa until after the battle. He went to collect
three totally hairy wounds for himself and whole slews of new notches on
his sword. Whoa *nelly*, life in the old fox yet, I'm sure.

So it was like that all morning and all afternoon: one surge after another,
dinking one part of our lines and then another. We met each charge,
though, and the shouting and clanging of swords and the death-cries of
Union and Confederate dudes were fully ready to drive me dizzy. There
was nothing to do but hang in there and put up a good fight, especially
when your *horse* wants to gallop into the heaviest part of the action, right,
and doesn't know the meaning of the word "retreat." I knew the meaning,
but Mr. Ed must have been absent the day they were teaching *that* one.

The Moon Maidens were our artillery all this time, but Milo couldn't
spare any infantry to like support them. They softened up the Ehleenee
with their arrow showers well before the enemy got into sword range, so
every rush up the side of the hills cost the Union plenty even *before* they
touched steel with us. As the sun set, *Strahteegos* Lahmbrohs, the Dim
Bulb, had a big part of his army like totally lying on their bellies all along
the ridge, really just yards from the Confederate positions. The Ehleenee
had gotten within feet—okay, within inches sometimes—of overrunning
our brave dudes, but every time, just at the maximum moment, the Union
rebels lost their drive, or the Confederate regulars and their Freefighter
pals found like a new hardness of will. At last, that part of Lahmbrohs's
strength was totally used up, and the men hung onto the side of the ridge,
waiting for dawn and another order to like attack.

But Lahmbrohs was not ready to call it quits just on account of *night* was
coming on, okay? He made one last push against the far right of the line,
like on Cemetery and Culp's Hills. That attack was more successful, like
they actually broke through the defense and charged into the unprotected
Moon Maidens. I was still mounted and ready, although I was about to like
rolf, for sure, I was so totally wasted. I didn't know if I could handle

another fight, but I go, "Maureen, honey, *go* for it, party hearty." Mr. Ed, bless her little heart, was right with me, so off we went to save Moon Maidens. I mean, they never so much as laid a "*hi*" on me before the battle, but I'm not one to like be all stuck-up about something like that, you know? Right.

Well, there was one furious fight in the twilight. The Moon Maidens stood their ground like good little girls, and pelted the Greeks with like a nonstop *hailstorm* of deadly arrows. A Pitzburker veteran told me like he'd never seen *anything* so terrible and bloody. I never even had a chance to use my sword—the Moon Maidens were skewering their attackers faster than reinforcements could get close. After a while there were no more Ehleenee willing to like stand up against those like *totally* excellent archers.

Night fell, but wouldn't you like know it?, I wasn't done yet. I was leading Mr. Ed down to a stream to water her, right, with four or five other tired Confederate buddies, and like we look up and on the other side of the water there's this lame bunch of Union men. So we went at it right there, hand-to-hand, and it didn't take long to totally *burn* those dudes. We didn't get one scratch among us. It was just like this pointless hassle that kept me from supper and had me fully edged, I'm sure.

There was a strategy meeting in Milo's tent, set up all secure behind our lines. Milo talked, we listened. He goes, "Tell your soldiers that they all did a fine job today, but the battle isn't over yet."

Prince Byruhn of New Kuhmbuhluhn goes, "Where do you think Lahm-brohs will hit us tomorrow?"

"He failed today on both flanks, again and again," Milo goes. "I am almost certain that he will concentrate on our center at dawn."

"He still has a couple of thousand men spread out on the face of Cemetery Hill," said *Strahteegos* Klaytuhn of Pitzburk.

"I haven't forgotten them. They won't get any sleep tonight, and they're exhausted. When the sun comes up, the fighting between your Freefighters and those weary Union boys will start up by itself. I don't expect they will stay in the battle very long. They are almost spent as it is."

So I go, "Then it's like the center I have to worry about, right?"

Milo gave me a warm smile. He goes, "Our center is where our best men are, covered by squadrons of Moon Maidens, in a solidly dug-in position, high uphill from the attacking Ehleenee."

"Pickett's Charge," I go, fully freaked but like *knowing* that it was coming all the time.

"Pickett's Charge," goes Milo.

I kind of remembered something I learned from Daddy. General Longstreet had told Robert E. Lee that no fifteen thousand men ever put on any battlefield in history could take our position. I was like really hoping he was right, you know?

The meeting ended a little after that, and then it was nighty-night, y'all.

Come the morning, Milo was like totally right about his first prediction: the Ehleenee on the hillside made these *completely* wimpy swipes at the Pitzburkers, then gave up and bailed, happy trails. They probably had the best chance of getting out of Gettysburg—I mean, Getzburk—alive or something, I don't know.

All that's left is the charge itself. I sat Mr. Ed in the center of our line. I could like hear the wailing voice of the bloody God of War in my head, but the God of War sounded just like, you know, that Freddy Mercury, the lead singer of Queen. First I could hear him doing "We will, we will *rock* you!" But it totally wasn't like any fun to watch what was going on. That's all we did, was *watch*. Like the Moon Maidens picked off every one of the poor bastards while they were crossing the low ground. Freddy Mercury shifted right into "Another one bites the dust." Suddenly like everything went *quiet*. None of our boys were shouting or anything, and you know none of the Ehleenee were in a mood to whoop it up, for sure. It was weird, the silence I mean, and I felt this creepy tingly feeling. I go, "Maureen like this is *so* ill." But there was nothing to do but watch. They kept coming on like lemmings, hustling their buns to suicide. "Gross, gross, *gross*," I go. They kept coming.

Then the Moon Maidens let fly, and the air was like totally filled with the zeeping of their bowstrings and the whooshing of the arrows. The Ehleenee hodads were coming through it in nice, straight lines, like they wanted to impress us with their *neatness*, I'm *so sure*. But the arrows punched gaps in their lines, more gaps every second as the Union lines marched nearer. As more of them went down, the Greeks who were like still alive like, you know, started to amble back to safety. They got punctured while they were retreating, too.

Then it was all over. Little Freddy was singing "We are the champions!" in my pea-brain. Maybe half of the Ehleenee were still alive, running for their lives. The Battle of Getzburk was like *history*, in more ways than one, like for sure. We watched them as they fled. Our boys were celebrating, and the commanders looked on, you know, *proudly* and all.

At supper, Milo came by to talk to me a little bit. He goes, "You were an inspiration to our men, Mahreenah."

I go, "It was like nothing, God-Milo."

"Will you go on with us? This battle is done, but there will be many more before the war is won."

I like chewed my lip, pretending to think about it. "Milo," I go at last, "there are many worlds and many oppressed peoples, and it is my sacred duty like to *stand up* for the little clods whenever they're being, you know, like forced to eat *dirt*."

"I understand. I wish you well in your crusade."

"Thanks. And good luck to you." I didn't know what else to say, but I thought of a question. "Am I like, you know, *really* immortal?"

"You are in *this* universe. I can't say if you are anywhere else. Perhaps you're not truly traveling from world to world, but from parallel reality to parallel reality."

That made me think. I figured I better not try any crankin' heroics until I checked things out. I like didn't want to find out the *hard* way, right, that whoa! I'm *not* immortal on Venus or Ganymede or ancient Babylon if I turned up there. I ought to like test every place by socking myself in the nose and watching how long it takes to stop bleeding, I'm sure. I didn't know what to do, but Milo had planted a grody seed of doubt, you know?

I gave him this zingy salute, I go, "Seeyabye," and then I whooshed on out of there.

AND LIKE RIGHT INTO my honeymoon *suite. This is where you and I came in. Maureen came to the end of her story and she was totally right: I was amazed. I was also like still stunned from the sock on the jaw she gave me, which I am never, ever going to forget. I just put that on the bill with the heartache and suffering she'd caused me in the past. I'd collect on it all someday, for sure.*

She was going to climb out the bathroom window, but I stopped her. She goes, "What now?" like I've been making demands on her.

I go, "Maureen, you're still cruising the Solar System like some kind of kid on summer vacation. I mean, look at it—Maureen Birnbaum, Tacky Girl Beast. You're getting muscles, honey. If you start growing a mustache, you should seriously think about passing the heavy responsibility to someone else. A guy, maybe." She glowered at me like really threatening, but I held up a hand. "Look at me. Happily married Bitsy Spiegelman Fein, settled wife and planning maybe to be a mother, if you ever let me spend some time alone with Josh. Real adult stuff, real adult hopes and dreams. Who are you? Still Muffy Birnbaum, the One Woman Mercenary Army. It's not chic, *sweetie. It doesn't fit you at* all. *And you know what else doesn't fit? Look at us in the mirror. What do you see?"*

She goes, *"I see* you, *you zod, and me."*

I go, *"I see me, twenty-two years old. I see* you, *and you look the same as you did when you were a junior at the Greenberg School."*

She goes, *"I do?"*

I go, *"Uh huh."*

She goes, *"Whoa, get back! Maybe I really* am *immortal."*

I go, *"Maybe you really are a case of arrested development." I had to duck fast after that one. She grabbed her spear and her bag and everything and like thundered out of the bathroom. Too late I tried to stop her. "Muffy! No!" I yelled.*

She was already crossing the suite to the front door. My darling Josh was standing there in his boxer shorts, socks, and garter, holding two glasses of champagne. He had a peculiar look on his face. The front door slammed shut after Maureen. I looked back at Josh. He turned to me, trying to like make sense out of the apparition that escaped his bathroom. I go, "That was Muffy Birnbaum, sweetheart. You've heard me speak of her."

He goes, "Right."

I took one of the glasses from him and drained the champagne in one long gulp. I didn't mention Maureen again. What Josh didn't know wouldn't barf him out. Loose Lips Sink Ships, like I'm totally sure.

Isaac Asimov, it goes without saying, was a science fiction immortal, and it pleased me more than I can say when I was invited to write a story for an anthology called *Foundation's Friends,* a volume in tribute to the Good Doctor. The idea was to come up with a story set in one of the many worlds and futures Asimov created during his long career.

There were, naturally, a good many respectful robot and Foundation stories, but I decided to play around with "Nightfall," an early Asimov piece that has frequently been mentioned as the most famous science fiction short story ever written. I asked Isaac's permission to completely trash his classic tale. The postcard he sent to me after reading "Maureen Birnbaum after Dark" is testimony to his well-documented sense of humor.

Maureen Birnbaum
After Dark

Maureen Birnbaum
After Dark

by Betsy Spiegelman Fein

(as told to George Alec Effinger)

ABOUT TWO MONTHS *after she barged into my honeymoon with Josh, Maureen showed up again. My jaw no longer hurt where she'd cracked me, but I still recalled how nearly impossible it had been to explain to my new husband what this totally unkempt barbarian girl in chain mail was doing in our hotel suite. I mean, it was our wedding night and all. Josh had just carried me across the threshold, and I'd gone into the bathroom "to freshen up," and there she was, God's Gift to the Golden Horde, Muffy herself. She spooked Josh out of his socks when she stormed out of the bathroom and through the front door. Josh's jaw dropped to his knees, okay? I couldn't get his mind back on honeymoon activities for two or three hours. Maureen has caused me a lot of grief over the years, but spoiling my wedding night takes the cake. I was never going to speak to her as long as I lived.*

Only she showed up again with another of her crummy adventures. I was trying to make this strawberry cheese quiche from scratch for the first time. I went into the pantry to get something, and there she was. She likes to startle me, I think. Her idea of a cool joke. See, I'm twenty-two and settled now, but Maureen looks exactly the same way she did as a junior at the Greenberg

School. She thinks like a high school kid, too. So I give this little yipe of surprise when I see her, and then I go, "Out! Out!" She smiled at me like nothing weird had ever happened between us, and she came out of my pantry chewing on a handful of sugar-coated cereal. I frowned at her and go, "I didn't mean just out of the pantry. I want you out of the house, like now." I was edged, for sure.

"Hold on, Bitsy," she goes, "you haven't even heard my latest story."

"And I'm not Bitsy anymore," I go. "You don't want to be called Muffy, I don't want to be called Bitsy. I'm grown up now. Call me Betsy or Elizabeth. That's what Josh calls me. Elizabeth."

She laughed. "And where is dear Josh today? I don't want to totally blow him away again or anything."

"He's seeing patients this afternoon."

"Good," goes Maureen, "then you can knock off for a little while and listen."

"I'm not going to listen, sister. I've got work to do. Why don't you find a psychoanalyst to listen to you? It would do you like just so much good."

"Ha ha," she goes, ignoring everything I said to her. Then she started telling me this story whether I wanted to hear it or not, and I didn't want to hear it.

I think she thought we were still friends.

Y OU REMEMBER the last time I bopped by, I told you all about this battle in the far future I won like singlehanded, okay? So after I left you and your darling doctor hubby in Bermuda, I decided to whoosh on out of your honeymoon suite and try to find Mars again. Mars is, you know, my *destiny*, and where I met that totally bluff Prince Van. I was still drooling like a schoolgirl over him, and I'd been *dying* to run into him again. But I just kept missing Mars, and I couldn't figure out what I was doing wrong. Maybe it was my follow-through, or I wasn't keeping my head down or something. I just didn't understand how I was messing up.

Anyway, from down by your hotel's pool I aimed at Mars, but I landed someplace that didn't look anything like the part of Mars I knew: no ocher dead sea bottom, no hurtling moons, no bizarro green men. I jumped up and down a couple of times to see if maybe it felt like Martian gravity, but no such luck. Good ol' Maureen wasn't going to have any help carrying around her heroinely poundage here. Matter of fact, I was just a teensy bit heftier in this place than on Earth. Right off, I figured wherever this was, it wasn't going to make my short list of fave vacation spots. My *God*, like who needs a complimentary gift of an extra fifteen pounds to lug around, know what I mean?

I was disappointed, but so what else is new? If these thrilling exploits of mine have taught me one thing, it's that you can't always get what you want. Yeah, you're right, Bitsy, Mick Jagger said the same thing entire *decades* ago, but I don't get my wisdom from ancient song stylists of our parents' generation.

The first thing I do when I de-whoosh in one of these weirdo places is try to sort out the ground rules, 'cause they're always different. It pays to find out up front if you're likely to be scarfed down for lunch by some hairball monster, or worshiped as the reincarnation of Joan Crawford or something. Between you and me, sweetie, being worshiped is only marginally better than death, but we savage warrior-women won't accept *either* treatment. You must've learned *that* much from me by now, and I hope you've let your Josh know all about it.

Bitsy, can I get something to drink out of your fridge? I mean, I just got back from saving the civilization of an entire world from destruction, and I'm dying for a Tab. Jeez, you don't have any Tab, and you used to be Miss Diet Bubbles of Greater Long Island. And no *beer*, either! Whatever happened to Blitzy Bitsy Spiegelman, the original party vegetable? You've got five different brands of bottled water in here, and not a single one of them is Perrier! What, you serve one water with fish and another with meat? 'A pure, delicious water from the natural miracle of New Jersey's sparkling springs.' You drink water from *New Jersey*? Bitsy, are you like fully wheezed or what? Josh's idea, right?

So where was I? No, never mind, I'll just die of thirst. Anyway, I looked around and at first it didn't really seem like another planet or anything. I was standing in this road, okay? I was most of the way up a hill, and behind me the pavement wound down through these trees and stuff, and I could see a pretty big town down there. It reminded me a lot of this time Daddy and Pammy took me to Santa Barbara, except I couldn't see anything like an ocean from where I was on that hill. Up ahead of me was a big building with a dome on it, like one of those places where they keep their telescopes, you know? I can't remember what they call 'em, but you know what I mean. Well, the dome place was a lot closer than the city, so I started booking it up the road the rest of the way.

Now, at this point, the only evidence I had that I wasn't on Earth somewhere was my weight, and you've probably noticed that I've tended to bulk up just a smidge from one adventure to the next. So maybe, I think, I really *am* just outside of Santa Barbara or somewhere, and the extra fifteen pounds is like this horrible souvenir I picked up in The World of Tomorrow. I did have lots of healthful exercise there, bashing skulls in the fresh air, a diet that would lay Richard Simmons in his *grave*—I mean, *look* at these muscles! These lats would make Stallone jealous!

This is how I'm talking to myself, until I notice that there's a partial sunset going on off to the left. A *partial* sunset. That's where not all of the suns in the sky seem to be setting at the same time. See, there was this yellow sun plunking itself down on the horizon, and making a real nice show out of the mists in the valley, and ordinarily I would have stopped and admired it because sunsets are like *so* cute. Why do people get so totally poetic about sunsets, anyway? I mean, there's always another one coming, like buses, and they're all pretty much the same, too. You don't have *critics* reviewing sunsets. Today's will be just like yesterday's, and there's not much hope that tomorrow's will be any more special. So what's the big deal?

Well, even after the yellow sun faded away, it was still daytime, 'cause there was still this *other* little sun hanging around. I thought it might be the moon, except it was almost as bright as the sun that had set, and it was red. "Okay, Maureen," I go, "this is *not* Earth. And it's not even in the whatyoucall, the solar system. You *really* flaked out this time."

A couple of seconds later, I realized I was in big trouble. See, my interspatial whooshing depends on being able to see my goal in the heavens. That's how I got to Mars, remember? I stood out under the night sky and raised my beseeching arms to the ruddy God of War, and like whoosh! there I was. So, despite my steering problems, I've always found my way home 'cause I've always stayed sort of in the same neighborhood. Now, though, it was all different. I wasn't going to be able to see the Earth in the sky at all. And the sun—the *right* sun, *our* sun—would be just one bright dot lost among all the others. If it was even there at all.

But I hadn't been *entirely* abandoned by Fate. After all, I was only half a mile downwind from an observatory. They'd be able to point me in the right direction, I was sure of it.

I cranked uphill for a few minutes, starting to feel a little weirded out. The light from the small sun was the color of beet juice, and it kind of sluiced down over the trees and the road and made me look like I'd been boiled too long. I was just telling myself that I hoped no one would see me until I got inside the observatory, when I spotted this guy hustling down the road toward me.

"Great," I go, "he'll think I've been pickled in a jar or something." But there wasn't anything I could do about it, so I stopped worrying. After all, *his* color was halfway between a crabapple and an eggplant, too.

He wasn't a bad-looking guy, either, even though in that light he looked like the Xylocaine poster child. The only odd thing about him was his clothes. He had on a kind of silvery jumpsuit with those stupid things that stand up on your shoulders, like the visitors from the future always wore in old sci-fi movies. He looked like Superman's dad from back in the good old days on Krypton. "Oh boy," I go, "welcome to the World of Superscience."

I guess he was just as freaked to see me. I mean, I was wearing my working outfit, which was just the gold brassiere and G-string I picked up on my travels, with Old Betsy hung on my hip. Maybe it was the broadsword, or maybe he was just overcome by my ample figure, but he just came to a stop in the middle of the road and stared. I mean, if I whoosh through space in a drop-dead outfit I stumbled on at Lillie Rubin, I land in Fred Flintstone's backyard. If I slide into my fighting harness instead, it figures I end up in some totally tasteful garden party beyond the stars. You can't win, right?

Which reminds me, Bitsy. Every time I see you, you look like you need *intensive care* from the Fashion Resuscitators. Look at you now! Everything you're wearing is black or drab colors and loose and shapeless. And hightop gym shoes with black socks? *Bitsy!* Has the FBS Catalog lost your address, or *what?*

Never mind. I looked at this Luke Floorwalker and I figured it was time for an exchange of interplanetary greetings. I stepped forward and raised my hand in the universal sign of peace. "I come from a planet not unlike your own," I go, real solemn. "I am Maureen Danielle Birnbaum. Do not call me Muffy."

This dweeb just boggled at me with his mouth opening and closing like a *goldfish* or something. Finally he figured out how his mouthparts were connected, and he goes, "You've come much sooner than we expected."

"Excuse me?" I go. I hadn't fully realized that my reputation was spreading all through the universe.

"We didn't think there'd be any serious trouble until after totality," he goes.

"I'm no trouble," I go. "I come in peace for all mankind."

He took a couple of steps forward and looked a little closer at my garb.

He reached out with a finger to boink my chestal covering. Guys are always trying to do that to me. "Whoa, like men have died for less," I go, in my Command Voice.

"Forgive me, my dear girl. Your fall into barbarism was also more immediate than we predicted."

This goober *rapidly* needed straightening out. Old Betsy sang as I whipped her from her scabbard. "I'm *not* your dear girl, like I'm totally sure," I go. "And it's not barbarism or anything. It's like being fully wild and free."

"Whatever," he goes. "But let me introduce myself. I am Segol 154." He cocked his head to one side, so I was supposed to be impressed or something.

"Segol 154?" I go. "Is that like a name you spraypaint on subway cars? You live on 154th Street, or what?"

Now it was his turn to look bummed out. "I am Segol 154. That is my cognomination." He said it with this little grisly sneer.

"Well, forget *you*," I go. I just didn't like his attitude, you know?

He paid no attention. "May I ask you, how long have you been under this delusion?"

I go, "What delusion?"

He goes, "This belief that you're from another planet?"

Now, see, in every one of these doggone exploits there comes a time when I have to *prove* I'm from another planet. Sometimes it's hard and sometimes it's easy. So I go, "Why *can't* I be from another planet?"

Segol 154 just shook his head sadly. "Because there *are* no other planets. Lagash is all alone, circling Alpha. There are five other suns, but no planets. Although in the last ten years, the work of Aton 77 and others has deduced the existence of a lesser satellite, we're equally certain that no life could exist upon it."

"No other planets? Oh *yeah?*" Okay, so maybe I could've come up with a stronger argument.

"Yes, that is the case. So you see, you can't be from another planet. You were born on Lagash, just as I was."

"I never even *heard* of Lagash until a minute ago! I came from Earth, that beautiful sapphire-blue world my people so sadly take for granted."

"If that is the case," he goes, smirking like an idiot, "how do you explain the fact that you speak English?"

Well, I've told you before, it's just amazing, huh? No matter where my adventures take me, they speak English when I get there. Prince Van spoke

66

English on Mars, and the ape-things in the center of the Earth spoke English, and they were still speaking English in the far distant future. So I guess it was no biggie to find out they spoke English on Lagash, too. But I wasn't going to tell Segol about all that. "I have studied your language," I go. "We've picked up your television programs on Earth for some time, okay?"

His eyes kind of narrowed, and he looked at me for a little while without saying anything. Then he goes, "What is television?"

Omigod! Like I'm on a weirdo planet *with no TV!* "Your radio broadcasts," I go, "that's what I meant. We've studied your language and learned many things about your culture and all."

He nodded. "It's possible," he goes. "There are many questions I must ask you, before I can be sure you are speaking the truth. But we can't talk here. You must come with me. I was on my way to the Hideout."

Now, believe me, at first I thought he was a complete dudley, but I've learned to give guys the benefit of the doubt. You never know who's got like, you know, a cute little ski shack in Vail or something. So I didn't bail on this guy just 'cause he looked like he probably bit the heads off chipmunks in his bedroom or something, and anyway he'd just invited me to cruise the local Lagash nightlife.

I turned around in front of him and I go, "So am I dressed for the Hideout, or what? Is there dancing, or are we just going to like, you know, sit there and *drink* all night?" Which would've been okay, too. We warrior-women can party till our brass brassieres turn green.

Segol looked at me like I was whoa nelly crazy or something. "What are you talking about?" he goes. "We're in terrible danger here. The Hideout is our only chance of survival. We have to hurry!"

Okay, I'm not as stupid as I look: I finally figured out that the Hideout was like a *hideout* or something. We started hurrying back down the road. "Where *is* this place?" I go. "And what are you so afraid of?"

"It's going to be dark soon," he goes, as if that said it all.

I laughed. "Your mama wants you home by suppertime, huh?"

"My dear girl—" He saw the grim look in my eyes and caught himself. "Maureen, perhaps you haven't heard Aton's ideas explained clearly."

I go, "So who *is* this Aton dude when he's at home? You mentioned him before."

"Aton 77 is one of the most brilliant scientists on all of Lagash. He is a famous astronomer, and director of Saro University. He's predicted that the entire world will go mad tonight when total Darkness falls."

It sounded mondo dumb to me. "That's why God gave us nightlights," I go. "I mean, I even had this Jiminy Cricket lamp when I was a kid. Wouldn't go to sleep or *anything* until Daddy turned it on for me."

His voice trailed off. I don't think he even heard me, you know? He goes, "And then after the insanity starts, the fire and destruction will begin. Nothing will be left. Our entire civilization, every vestige of our culture, *all* of it will be eradicated. And the Observatory will be the first target, thanks to the Cultists. Our only hope is the Hideout."

I slid Old Betsy back into her scabbard while I thought about what Segol had said. "You're not kidding about this," I go. "You're like *really* scared, huh?"

He dropped his gaze to the ground. "I admit it," he goes, "I'm terrified."

Well, jeez, Bitsy, he was like such a little boy when he said that! I couldn't help but feel sorry for him, even though I still figured he was maybe stretching the truth just a teensy bit. "That Aton guy is still up there at the Observatory, right?" I go.

Segol looked up at me sort of mournfully. "Yes, along with a few of the other scientists who volunteered to stay behind and record the event."

"And you were supposed to be there, too?"

He looked ashamed, but all he did was nod his head.

"And instead, you're just zeeking out and lamming it for the Hideout."

"We've got to move fast, because they'll be coming from Saro City. They may kill us if they catch us here!"

I had this picture in my mind of those clearly freaked villagers waving torches around in Frankenstein, you know? I knew I could save this guy from a dozen or two rousted locals, but if the whole city turned up, whoa, like seeyabye! So the Hideout sounded like a maximum cool idea.

We followed the road downhill, and I had more time to think about what Segol had said. I mean, either the deadly cold of deep space had frozen my brain, or I was like *really* missing something. All I knew was that a lot of irked people were going to shred the Observatory, because they'd be driven loony by the darkness. See, I hadn't noticed the capital D Segol had put on "Darkness."

"Mr. 154," I go, "or may I call you Segol? Can I like ask you something?"

"Huh?" he goes. He was way spaced, and he wasn't even paying attention to me or anything.

"What makes this night different from all other nights?" I go. There was this moment of quiet when I realized that I sounded just like my little cousin Howard on Passover at my Uncle Sammy's. Maybe I'd heard Segol wrong. Maybe he said the threat was coming from *"Pharaoh* City," not *"Saro* City."

"Why, nothing," he goes. "Aton's warning is that tonight will be exactly like last night, two thousand years ago. That's the terrible truth."

"You want me to believe it hasn't been dark in two thousand years? I mean, when do you people *sleep?* Look, Lagash would have to practically creep around on its whatyoucall for the days to be that long. And then imagine what it would be like for the poor people on the dark side, going to the beach in the pitch dark all the time." The whole idea was like too weird for words.

He goes, "I can almost believe that you've come here from some other world. Lagash turns once about its axis in a little more than twenty-three hours. Our nearly eternal day is caused by the six suns. There is always at least one in the sky at all times."

"Six?" I go. "Now that's just *too* flaky. If you had *that* many up there, they'd be blamming into each other all the time."

He just gave me his indulgent, superior little smirk again. "I see that you aren't familiar with celestial mechanics," he goes.

"And like you probably aren't familiar with anything *else,*" I go. I could tell by his expression that I'd really ranked him out.

"The perpetual presence of one or more suns in the skies of Lagash means that Darkness falls only once every 2,049 years, when five of the suns have set and the invisible moon passes between us and Beta, the only remaining source of light and warmth." He glanced upward, and I saw him freeze in terror. Already, the edge of the moon had dented the ruddy edge of Beta.

"Don't pay any attention to that," I go. I was trying to lend him some of my inexhaustible store of courage. But it was like *odd,* you know? There are all these stories on Earth about lucky explorers saving their lives by using eclipses to scare the natives. I had to do just the opposite. If the mindless mob caught us, I had to pretend that I could *end* the eclipse.

"Soon," he goes, "the Stars!"

"You bet," I go. I didn't see what all the excitement was. Of course, I didn't hear the capital letter again.

"When the Stars come out, the world will come to an end." He looked at me, and his eyes were all big and bugged out. I hated to see him so scared, okay? Even in that cranberry light he was sort of cute—for a brainy type, I mean. He wasn't Prince *Van* or anything, but he wasn't any Math Club geek, either.

"And you blame it all on the stars?" I go.

"Strange, isn't it? That Aton's warning should agree with the Cult? Believe me, he wasn't happy about it, but he's absolutely sure of his conclusions. There is definite proof that nine previous cultures have climbed to civilization, only to be destroyed by the Stars. And now it is our turn. Tomorrow, the world will belong to savages and madmen, and the long process will begin again."

I tapped him on the skull. "Hello, Segol?" I go. "Is anybody like *home?* You haven't told me what the stars have to do with it."

He wasn't really paying attention to me, which just goes to show you how zoned out he was, 'cause I made a pretty dramatic presentation with my boobs clad in a metal Maidenform and my broadsword and everything. He goes, "Beenay 25 had an insane idea that there might be as many as two dozen stars in the universe. Can you imagine?"

"Beenay 25?" I go. "It sounds like an acne cream."

"And the Stars, whatever they are, only come out in the Darkness. I think it's all superstitious hogwash, myself. But Aton believes that the Cult's ravings may have some basis in fact, that their *Book of Revelations* may have been written shortly after the *last* nightfall—"

Bitsy, you know how they say "my blood ran cold"? The orthodontist shows his bill to your parents and like their blood runs *cold*, okay? Well, right then I learned what they meant. It took a whole long time to seep into my brain, but finally I realized like, hey, if night falls only once every two thousand years around this place, then the stars won't come out again for *centuries,* right? And without stars, I'd never be able to whoosh myself home! I'd be stuck on Lagash *forever and ever!* And I already knew they didn't have TV, so that meant they also didn't have any of the other trappings of modern civilization that are dependent on TV, like the Shopping Channel and Lorenzo Lamas. And could the Galleria have existed back in those pre-test pattern dark ages? I think not.

So I was not going to be hanging out on Lagash long enough to find out what the dawn would bring. I had one window of opportunity, and I wasn't going to miss it. "What about the weather?" I go.

"Hmm?" Like Segol the Bionic Brain was aware of my existence again.

"You know, if it gets all cloudy, we won't be able to *see* the stars." Then I'd be trapped there for good.

He brightened up considerably for a moment. "Yes," he goes, "that would be a miracle."

"Not for *some* of us," I go. First I thought he'd fallen desperately in love

70

with me and wanted me to stay on Lagash. But this bozo was thinking that after two thousand years of buildup, the big night might come and it would be too overcast to see anything. *Quel* irony, right?

N.S.L., sweetie—No Such Luck. Beta, the red sun in the sky, was now only a thin crescent like a bloody sliver of fingernail or something. It wouldn't be much longer to total Darkness. It was like slightly obvious that we'd never make it to the Hideout in time. I was stuck out on this road with Segol 154, who was like a total loon. Still, the Hideout was all he could think about.

"We've got to hurry," he goes, putting his grubby hands on my person and kind of dragging me along after him. "We've got to get to the Hideout. We must make sure you're safe. Your destiny is to have babies, *many* babies, who will be the hope of Lagash's future."

I disenhanded myself from him and laughed, a proud and haughty laugh meaning "If you weren't such a pitiful *knob*, I'd hack you to little pieces for that remark." Let me tell you a little secret, honey: No matter where you go in the known universe, the men are all the same. It's like these honkers are what God gave us as *substitutes* because all the really buf guys are on back order.

So what does he do? He grabs me by both shoulders and goggles into my face. "You . . . will be . . . the mother of . . . my children!" he goes. And even if there wasn't a line of drool down his chin, like there should have been.

You know and I know—and, *believe* me, Bitsy, now this Segol knows—*nobody* paws me uninvited. I didn't care if civilization was quickly coming to a screeching halt. I was now totally bugged, and I was going to teach him a lesson in interspatial etiquette. I put one hand flat against his chest and pushed real hard, and the next thing he's down in the road squinting up at me all surprised. I whipped Old Betsy from her scabbard again and took a menacing step toward him. "Look!" he screams. "Behind you!"

"Oh, like I'm so sure," I go. But I heard these grumbly sounds, and I turned and saw a mob of people huffing up the hill toward us. They did not look pleased.

Segol scrabbled to his feet and stood beside me. "Let me do the talking, little lady," he goes. "They may still listen to reason. And maybe you'd better put that silly sword away."

I decided to let him take his shot. I didn't even freak out about being called "little lady." I was absolutely *beyond* arguing with him. He could try talking to the mob, and when he'd said his piece, I was going to lop his grody head off. Okay, like I'd given him fair warning, hadn't I?

But he wasn't even aware that he'd bummed me out. He started walking toward the crowd from the city, both hands raised above his head. I don't know what that was supposed to mean. Segol probably thought he was one dangerous dude. Maybe he thought that with his hands in the air, he wouldn't look like such a terrible threat to the safety of those five hundred howling maniacs. "Listen to me!" he goes. "Listen to me! I mean you no harm!"

Yeah, right. That made the mob feel a whole lot better about everything, for sure.

There was this raspy guy at the front of the crowd. He looked like he'd been getting ready for the end of civilization for a long time now, and like he couldn't wait for it to happen, you know? He had wild scraggy hair and big popping old eyes. He just about had a bird when he recognized Segol 154. "That's one of them!" he goes, waving his arms around a lot. "He's from the Observatory!"

Segol gave him this smile that was supposed to calm him down or something. "Come," he goes, "let us reason together."

"They didn't come here to *talk*," I go. "They came here to work your butt."

Someone else in the crowd started shouting, "Death to the unbelievers! Death to the blasphemers in the Observatory!"

That cry was taken up by others until it became this ugly chant. I wanted to tell them, hey, I'd never even *been* in the Observatory, but they wouldn't even have heard me.

Finally, a tall man in a black robe pushed his way to the front of the crowd. When he raised his hands, they all shut up. "Silence, my friends," he goes. "Let us give these profaners of the truth one last chance to redeem their souls."

"Who's that?" I go.

"His name is Sor 5," Segol goes. "He is the leader of the Cultists."

"Oh, huh," I go. I turned to this Sor 5 and I go, "I don't know anything about your Cult. What's your problem, anyway?"

The guy in the robe just gave me this sad little smile. "It's not *my* problem, young lady. It's yours. You have only a few minutes left before Lagash is swallowed up by the Cave of Darkness. Unless you embrace the revealed truth of our faith, your soul will be stripped from you when the Stars appear. You will become a savage, unreasoning brute."

I looked at the flipped-out people who made up his congregation, and I figured most of them didn't have far to go. Like maybe they'd already *seen* the stars, like at some kind of preview party or something. "So what are you guys selling?" I go.

Sor goes, "Behold! The Cave of Darkness is already engulfing Beta."

I looked up. There wasn't much of the red sun left. "Really," I go. "Tell me about it."

"Soon all will be in Darkness, and the Stars will blaze down in all their fury."

"Really."

Sor looked confused for a few seconds. "You do not deny any of this?"

I go, "See, you're telling me the same thing that Segol told me, and I can't figure out what your hang-up is."

That made him mad. I thought he was going to split his black robe. "We believe the Stars are the source of the Heavenly Flame, which will scourge and cleanse Lagash. The infidels of the Observatory insist that the Stars are nothing but burning balls of gas, physical objects like our own six suns. They refuse to grant that the Stars have any holy power at all."

"Death to the unbelievers!" screamed the mob. "Death to the blasphemers in the Observatory!" Sor tried again to quiet them, but this time they wouldn't listen. They surged forward, and I was like sure they were fully ready to tear us limb from limb. I brandished Old Betsy, but I backed away uphill, praying that Segol and I could somehow make it to the Observatory alive.

The astronomer shot me a terrified glance. "You hold them off," he goes, "and I'll run for help."

"Right," I go, sort of contemptuously, "you just do that." He was like a real poohbutt, you know?

Just then, the last red ember of Beta flickered in the sky and went out as the eclipse reached totality. There was a long moment of this really creepy quiet. You couldn't hear a sound, not a person gasping or an animal rustling, not even the wind. It was like being in a movie theater when the film breaks, just before the audience starts getting rowdy. And then the *stars* came out, normally No Big Deal.

Except on Lagash, it *was* a big deal, and not just 'cause it'd been two thousand years since the last time. Bitsy, these people really knew how to have *stars!* I looked up, and there were a zillion times as many stars as we have on Earth. It reminded me of when we were getting ready for that dance at Brush-Bennett, and you spilled that whole box of glitter on my black strapless. Remember? Well, on Lagash, the night sky looked just like that. All the places *between* the stars were crammed with stars.

"*Oh . . . my . . . God!*" I was totally impressed, but I wasn't, you know, going *insane* or anything.

"Stars!" goes Segol in this kind of strangled voice.

"Surprise," I go. I mean, he was a real melvin.

Now the mob started screaming and screeching and carrying on. They'd known the Stars were coming, but like they didn't have any idea what stars really *were*, or how *many* of them there'd be, and all that. So even Sor looked haired, but I give him credit, he pulled himself together pretty fast. "Our salvation will be the destruction of the Observatory," he goes. I mean, he couldn't bring himself to look up at the stars anymore, and he had to kind of croak his speech out, but he made himself heard. "If we destroy the Observatory and everyone in it, the Stars will spare us. And we must begin with them."

He was pointing at me and Segol. "That is *so* lame," I go. "Don't be stupid. There's nothing to be—"

Sadly, I didn't have the time to finish my explanation. The crowd was full-on crazy and ready to roust. When they charged, I felt a sudden calmness flood through me. I didn't know *what* Segol was doing and I didn't care. Old Betsy whistled through the air as I hacked and hewed at the waves of shrieking lunatics. Bodies piled up in front of me and on both sides. I took a couple of biffs and bruises, but I was too skillful and like too excellent for them to fight through my guard.

Of course, they had me outnumbered, and after a while I realized I was way tired. I wasn't going to be able to handle *all* of them, so while I fought I tried to think up some, you know, *strategy*. And then I saw their leader over on the side of the road, kneeling down in the dark, with his face turned up to the sky where the eclipse was still chugging along and the stars were still blazing away. I started working my way toward him, wading through his nutty buddies with my broadsword cutting a swath before me.

Finally I was right beside him. I reached down and grabbed him by the neck of his robe and jerked him to his feet. "I am Sor!" he goes, like frothing a little in the corners of his mouth. He wasn't all there anymore, okay?

"*You're* sore," I go. I let him go and he fell in a heap at my feet. "Tell your fruitcake army to stand still and shut up, or I'll split your skull open and let the starlight in."

Sor stared at me fearfully for a few seconds. Then he got to his feet and raised his arms. "Stand still and shut up!" he goes.

All the rest of the mob stopped what they were doing, which was mostly climbing over the stacks of bodies, trying to get to me.

"Good," I go. "You have no reason to be afraid."

Segol started babbling. I'd wondered what had happened to him. "Beenay guessed a dozen, maybe two dozen Stars. But this! The universe, the stars, the *bigness!*"

"Lagash is nothing, a speck of dust!" cried a voice from the mob.

"We're nothing but insects, *less* than insects!"

"I want light! Let's burn the Observatory!"

"We're so small, and the Darkness is so huge! Our suns and our planet are insignificant!"

Well, these people had a serious problem. All of a sudden, they realized that there was a lot more to the universe than their precious Lagash. Then I had an idea that might keep these frenzied folks from trashing *all* of their civilization and maybe save my own neck, too.

I go, "There's no reason to be afraid. The stars are not what you think. I *know.* I come from a world that has studied them for many centuries."

"She's mad! The Stars have driven her insane!"

"Listen to her!" Segol goes. "She told me the same story long before the Stars appeared. She speaks the truth."

"Yes," I go, "there *are* other stars in the universe. That's just something you're going to have to learn to live with. But not as many as *that.*" I pointed up, and noticed that the eclipse had moved on past totality, and a teeny tiny thread of red light was starting to grow on one side of Beta.

"Then what are all those thousands of points of light?" goes Sor.

"Tonight is a night for revelations and strange truth," I go. I'm always pretty good in a crisis like that. I can talk my way out of *anything.* Hey, *you* know that. You were my roommate, right? "Lagash, your six suns, and the other twelve stars in the universe are surrounded by a huge ball of ice."

"Ice?" goes Segol. He sounded like he was having just a little bit of trouble buying it.

"Sure, *ice,*" I go, acting kind of ticked off that he doubted me. "What did you think, that the universe just sort of went on and on *forever?* That's so *real,* I'm totally sure."

"A wall of ice," Sor goes. "The *Book of Revelations* speaks of a Cave of Darkness. I don't see why there can't be a wall of ice as well."

Now everyone had stopped trying to grab me by the throat. They were

all like hanging on my every word, okay? "But what *are* the Stars?" someone goes.

"The Stars are an illusion," I go. "What you see up there are only the
reflections of the dozen real stars, shining on the craggy ice wall of the
universe."

There was this silence. I held my breath 'cause everything would be
totally cool if they believed me, but I'd have to start fighting for my life
again if they didn't. Five seconds passed, then ten. Then all at once they all
went "Ahhhh."

Sor goes, "It's the divine truth!" I saw tears running down his face.

"Look!" goes Segol. "Beta! It's coming back!"

Sor waved his arms around and got their attention. "Let's hurry back to
Saro City," he goes. "We can spread the news and keep our brothers and
sisters from burning our homes. The other suns will rise in a few hours, and
then life must go on as before. We must tell the others what we've learned,
and broadcast the information to everyone on Lagash." Then they turned
and marched away, without so much as a thank-you.

When we were alone again on the road, Segol came over to me. He had
this big, spazzy grin on his face. "That was really something, my dear," he
goes.

"My name's *Maureen,* and this is the *last* time I'm going to remind you.
If you have trouble remembering that, you can call me Princess." Well,
Bitsy, I *know* I was sort of stretching the truth, but sometimes I liked to
think of myself as sort of almost engaged to Prince Van of the Angry Red
Planet. I mean, a woman's reach should exceed her grasp, or what's a mixer
at Yale for?

"Then congratulations, Maureen. You were outstanding. You have saved
us from centuries of Dark Ages. I think you'll always be remembered in the
history books of Lagash."

I shrugged. "What can I say?" I go. "It's like a gift."

Segol nodded, then hung his head in shame. "I guess I owe you an
apology, too. I wasn't much help to you during the battle."

"'S all right," I go. "You weren't really ready for all those stars." I was
just being gracious, you know? I'd been a little zoned out, too, when I saw
how many there were, but *I* got over it.

He looked back up at me, as grateful as that awful Akita puppy Daddy
brought home for Pammy's birthday. "Perhaps you'd permit me the honor,"
he goes, "of asking for your hand in marriage."

I was like too stunned to say anything for a moment. I wiped Old Betsy off on this dead guy's shirt and slid her slowly back into the scabbard. Then I go, "No, I won't permit you the honor of having my hand in *anything*. Nothing personal, okay?"

He was disappointed, of course, but he'd live. "I understand. Would you answer a question, then?"

"Sure, as long as it's not like way lewd or demeaning to all women."

He took a deep breath and he goes, "Is it *true?* What you told the Cultists? Is it true that Lagash is in the center of a gigantic ball of ice?"

I laughed. I mean, how megadumb could he be? I wasn't surprised that Sor 5 and his crowd swallowed that story, but I didn't think a real astronomer would buy it. Then I realized that this was *not* the World of Superscience, after all, and that Segol was just a poor guy trying to understand like the laws of nature and everything. I couldn't bring myself to weird him out any more than he already was. "Right, like totally," I go. "Maybe someday your own Observatory will figure out the distance from Lagash to the ice wall. I *used* to know, but I forgot."

"Thank you, Maureen," he goes. Suddenly he'd gotten so humble it was *ill*. "I think we'd better hurry back to tell Aton and the others the news. Beenay and the rest of the photographers should have captured the Stars with their imaging equipment. They were all prepared, of course, but even so they may have given way to panic." He looked down at the ground again, probably remembering how *he'd* bugged out of there in panic even *before* the stars came out.

"I'm sorry, Segol," I go. "I *can't* go back to the Observatory with you. I'm needed elsewhere. I've got to flash on back to Earth. If I wait much longer the eclipse will be over, the sky will get light, the stars will go out for another two thousand years, and I'll never see my dear, dear friend Bitsy *ever again.*" Sure, sweetie, even in this moment of awful tension, I thought of you. You *believe* me, don't you?

Segol sighed. "I suppose you must go, then. I'll never forget you, little la —I mean, Maureen."

I gave him this sort of *noblesse oblige* smile, but I stopped short of getting all emotional and everything. "Farewell, Segol 154," I go. "Tell the others that someday, when you've proved yourselves worthy, my people will welcome yours into the Federation of Planets. Until then, one last word of advice: Try to discourage anyone who starts fiddling around with radio astronomy. I think it will make you all very, *very* unhappy."

"Radio astronomy?" he goes. "How can you look at space with a radio?"

"Never mind, just remember what I said." I raised one hand in the universal sign of "That's all, folks." Then I raised my supplicating arms to the stars, went *eeny meeny miney mo*, and whooshed myself on out of there.

I'M SORRY I had to listen to the whole story. By the time Maureen finished it, we had finished off all the strawberries, and a quiche with nothing in it is like tortellini salad without the tortellini. In the months that Josh and I had been together, he'd taught me a lot about food and everything. We didn't have supper anymore, we dined. And then like I did the dishes.

Anyway, it was getting late, and you know I had to rush her out of there, and I tried to explain to her but she just didn't want to listen, so then I put my back against her and shoved her toward the door, and I guess she got annoyed or something 'cause then I shoved some more but she wasn't there and I fell on the kitchen floor and she was standing over me with her sword in her hand and she had on what she called her warrior-woman expression, and I could just see the headlines in the Post: QUEENS WOMAN DIES IN SHISH KABOB TRAGEDY. *Josh would never be able to face our folks again. So I go, "Back off, Muffy." Wrong thing to say.*

"You're as bad as those ape-things in the center of the Earth!" She was screeching now.

I go, "Just bag your face, will you? Some roommate you are. Where's that old Greenberg School bond we used to have?" That got to her. She sheathed her jeweled sword and calmed down. She helped me get up and dusted me off a little. "I'm sorry, Bitsy," she goes. I noticed she was blushing.

"All right, I guess," I go. We looked at each other a little longer, then I started to cry for some reason, and then she trickled a couple, and we started hugging each other and bawling, and the front door opened and I heard Josh coming in, and all he needed was another unexplained visit from his favorite Savage Amazon, so I go, "Maureen, quick, you've got to hide!" And then I felt like we were all on I Love Lucy *or something, and I started to laugh.*

She laughed, too. Josh didn't laugh, though. Sometimes it's like we only see his friends, and why can't I ever have my friends over? Josh goes, "Because my friends don't wave broadswords around on the subway." I suppose he has a point there.

The following story I wrote for *The Fantastic Adventures of Robin Hood,* edited by Martin H. Greenberg (no relation to Muffy's alma mater). The book was a tie-in with the Kevin Costner film. As usual, I tried to steer clear of what I thought some other authors might attempt—here are no singlestick competitions, no flights of feathered clothyard shafts, no roistering beneath the sheltering boughs of Sherwood. I did a lot of research for this story, and now I know what a placket is, even if I don't particularly care.

Maureen Birnbaum
Goes Shopynge

Maureen Birnbaum
Goes Shopynge

by Elizabeth Spiegelman-Fein

(as told to George Alec Effinger)

I
T HAD BEEN a couple of years since I'd seen Maureen ("Muffy")
Birnbaum, and the time had passed in quiet, domestic bliss, sort
of. The old Mufferoo tended to insert herself into my life like a
migraine headache, and then leave suddenly, and in-between I
forgot how awful it was having her around. And now she had this
gigantic broadsword that she threatened you with if you called her by her
old nickname. I was her favorite target because we'd been roommates together back at the old Greenberg School. One of the migrainish things about
Maureen was that she still looked like a high school junior, while I was now
a twenty-six-year-old married woman.

Something else annoying about Maureen was that every single time she
showed up, she'd just finished some bizarre adventure on another planet or
somewhere, and she had to tell me all about it. It started off with Mars.
She'd whooshed off to Mars and killed a bunch of monsters and things, and
fell in love with this absolutely def—did I use that right? Part of being
twenty-six is losing track of what the kids are doing to the language—prince.
She'd been trying ever since to get back to Mars and Prince Van, but her
steering component failed her regularly. And she refused to notice that I had

a life, too, even if it was just a fern-filled apartment in Queens and a shelf of Richard Simmons aerobics tapes.

Another thing that I just like really hated was that I was now a married woman, and my hard-working Josh, when he wasn't seeing patients, didn't want to have to hear about Muffy's latest exploit—he didn't really like her, and could you blame him? Somewhere in one of these stories I recorded how she'd made her grand entrance during our honeymoon night. I used to be called Bitsy, but in the last nine years I'd become Elizabeth to everybody but certain members of my family whom I couldn't re-educate. And lately Josh and I had hyphenated our names in honor of the baby that was due in another four months. We just didn't have much in common with Miss Birnbaum anymore.

So things were going along just fine, with me sweating to the oldies and sharing the pre-natal experience with Josh, when one afternoon when my husband was out communicating the golf experience with some professional men in his building, who should whoosh into my nice, clean kitchen but Muffy—I mean Maureen—Birnbaum. It was migraine time, and before I said a word to her, I went into the bathroom and took some of the pharmaceutical requisites Josh had left around for just such an emergency.

"Don't I look nice?" asked Muffy. "Tell me I don't look nice."

Well, she did look nice, dressed like a normal grown person instead of wearing the science-fiction magazine cover outfits she usually schlepped around in. "You look terrific, Maureen," I said. "You lost a little weight, maybe?" This is never true when one woman says it to another. It was just part of the getting-older ritual that I'd learned. Maureen had missed all that, spending her time adventuring God-knows-where.

"They wrapped my things for me. Old Betsy—the broadsword—and the gold brassiere, and the dagger and everything else. Didn't they make a nice package out of it?"

I was afraid to say "Who made a nice package out of it?" because that would only lead into the latest exploit, but before I could say anything, she started in without a molecule of encouragement from me.

I MAGINE MY SURPRISE when I whooshed back to earth from Lagash to find myself in Merrie Olde England. I half-expected myself to end up in the New York Transit System, as I usually do, but not this time. I knew it was London because there were these big red buses and everybody talked funny. I'll just leave in the buses and leave out the funny talking, because it got to be really boring and tedious and a lot like the Dave Clark Five after a while, and who wants to sound like the Dave Clark Five? I usually whoosh back here, or around here, but there I was in London. The great thing about London, aside from all the historic things you can see, is that I landed right near a mall. A mall like we have here, with a food court and silly things hanging from the ceiling, but strange shops you've never heard of.

Well, I could've gone to the British Museum, I suppose, or the Tower of London, but there was this mall right in front of me. And it was called the Sherwood Forest Mall, because apparently they'd torn the forest down a long time since, and put in freeways—which they call motorways—and yogurt shops and what-all. So I sort of sauntered into the Sherwood Forest Mall, wearing my metal bikini and armed to the teeth. Nobody seemed to notice, either, which was kind of strange.

I walked around the mall for a while, and it was just a bum, Bitsy, I mean, there were only jeans shops and record stores and the usual. I was ready to H. T. P.—hit the pavement, you know? Then I met this nice couple at a newsstand. We were checking out what was happening in each other's country; I wanted to know what was going on in Great Britain, and they wanted to know what was buzzing in the States. We got to talking, and the next thing we knew, we decided to go upstairs and have some lunch. Lunch in England is really hitting, if you check out the right places. In the Sherwood Forest Mall, there were only two good places, a fish-and-chips place that I wanted to give a miss to, and a cute little teashop like we don't have over here. I voted for the teashop, and since I had the broadsword, I won.

We were just lamping out in front of the teashop, talking, and I introduced myself. "My name is Maureen Birnbaum, interstellar adventuress," I go. The guy, who was totally buff—goes "And I am Robin Hood, and this babe-o is Maid Marian. Perhaps our reputations have crossed the great water?"

"Robin Hood?" I go. "*The* Robin Hood. The arrow in the center of the target guy, the enemy of the Sheriff of Nottingham and all bad heinies like that?"

He blushed, but the crushin' girl spoke up. "Yup," she goes, "that's us."

Maybe I should have asked to see Robin or Marian's ID before we started out on this venture. "But I thought you lived like entire centuries ago," I go.

"As long as there is a Sherwood Forest and evildoers about, we're sort of immortal," goes Robin Hood.

"But there isn't any Sherwood Forest."

Maid Marian shrugged. "There was a jankin' bunch of trees before you came into the mall, wasn't there?"

You could hear my jaw drop. "*That's* Sherwood Forest?"

"What's left of it," goes Robin Hood.

"What about the Merrie Men?" I spelled "Merry" in my mind the olde way, to honor the gang.

"They're down by the Video Arcade," goes Robin Hood. "You should see Little John on the flipper tables."

"Little John!" I go. This *was* Robin Hood. "Like I've always wanted to meet you. See, I'm like this barbarian hero-type, and I've always wondered how I'd measure up to a real hero like you. Maybe we could have a contest or something."

"Well," goes Robin Hood, stroking his well-trimmed beard, "longbow archery is like out, because that's my big thing."

"Right," I go.

"But we could singlestick across a log; I've been beaten at that before. Or we could try pikes or—"

"No, no, even at your best, I think I'd have the advantage over you," I go. "You don't know the adventures I've had and the victories I've like won."

"Well, if you think so," goes Robin Hood, kind of sourly I thought.

"I know," goes Maid Marian. "How about a shopping duel, right here in the mall!"

"Lady," I go, "I was *born* to shop. You've never seen an American, pride-full-of-country, all together in patriotic merchandising splendor."

"I have no fear of foreign economic imperialism," goes Maid Marian. "I come from a very well-to-do family. The Monceux clan; perhaps you've heard of it?"

"No," I go, "I'm afraid not. Do you have an acquaintance with the Birnbaums? The New York Birnbaums?"

"A shopping duel it is, then," goes Robin Hood. "There shall be three events: a formal outfit; a normal daily outfit; and casual attire. I have no doubt that my Maid Marian will triumph in all three."

"Well," I go, "if there's one thing I know, it's clothesisimo."

"Couldn't tell it from the costume you're wearing now," goes Maid Marian.

"It's not much to look at," I go, "but it's serviceable and just what the contemporary female barbarian is wearing these days."

Maid Marian goes, "It's well past noon. We should meet back here about twoish with the formal outfit? And then fourish with the daily clothes? And then sixish with the casual attire. Then we can have dinner here in this tea shop."

"Two hours each?" I go. "To shop for three complete outfits?"

"It's a duel," goes Robin Hood. "Let the time limit be a part of the challenge."

"That's fat, then," I go. "I'll go along with whatever you say."

"And no like sneaking out of the mall to find some better shops," goes Maid Marian.

"Pretty dopey, Marian," I go, and I head off to see what the Sherwood Forest Mall had in the way of clothing stores.

After passing a lot of typical women's wear stores, I found a pretty classy place called Rhodes and Maxwell. You could tell they were exclusive because the mannequins in the windows only had half a head each. I went into the shop, not thinking in the least of how I was mostly undressed. The fashion coordinator—in America she would have been a saleslady—approached me as if I were just another matron coming in looking for a ball gown. She pretended not to notice Old Betsy, my trusty broadsword, or any of the rest of my tough, fierce raiment. "Yes?" she goes. "May I help you?"

I liked her a lot for her spirit, which was a typically British attitude, as I was to find out.

"Well, I wanted a real ass-kicking formal thing. Something to wear to a princess's wedding or something?"

"A Yank are we?" she goes, smiling. "Get invited to a lot of princess's weddings, do we?"

"Never mind about that. Let's see what you've got. The more expensive the better." Fashion coordinators around the world like to hear that.

"Good answer!" she goes, showing that American television gets distributed pretty widely. I could probably have gotten the same response in Sri Lanka. She began pulling things out of drawers, not off the racks. "How's this?" she goes.

87

The third dress she selected was classic yet glamorous. It was sewn together out of Imperial blue faux-silk, with a V-neckline that would require a serious, strapless, longline, underwired bra, which I'm sure she'd be able to sell me, too. It had overlapping layers of fringe all the way down to the floor-length hemline. She showed me some simple accessories—opera-length faux pearls and matching Imperial blue pumps with a knot of more faux pearls. We found a faux pearl-covered handbag to complete the outfit. I figured I was real costing and definitely "Get up!" It cost me a fortune, but I was playing against a mythical figure, and you got to go with what you know in that kind of semi-fabricated situation.

"Would you care to wear this now, or shall I wrap it for you?" she goes.

I go, "I'll wear it now. I want to impress all the hanks here in the mall. Is this *really* Sherwood Forest? I'd pictured it as more than three mighty oaks and a few poozley rhododendrons."

She shrugged without replying, and very casually took my golden brassiere and spangled G-string, my dagger and broadsword, and folded them over in nicely patterned paper as if they were everyday items of nine-to-five apparel. I paid her with my father's credit card, which I kept under the G-string. She didn't hesitate for a minute; I gave her full marks for her entire deportment and general zoiks. I walked out of Rhodes and Maxwell feeling as if Maid Marian would have to go some to joan me out.

Well, unfortunately, Maid Marian had the secret knowledge of the Sherwood Forest Mall geography, and she *did* joan me out. She showed up at the teashop at two o'clock, wearing, I swear, something you might wear as a visiting monarch among yam-eating natives somewhere. She walked gracefully, on Robin's arm, because someone as formal as she required an escort. "Get up, girl!" he goes. Even Robin Hood had a new outfit—or an old one, the one you picture him in, in Lincoln green.

But Maid Marian! I was ready to toss in the towel, the washcloth, and the dishrag all at the same time. She showed up in a gown from Whitley's, which apparently is open only by appointment, but celebrities like Robin Hood and Maid Marian have permanent appointments. She was wearing a white chiffon gown lined with white satin, hand-beaded, of course. Gold—possibly *real* gold—and white bugle beads dropped in bunches from the waist to the hem in the shape of what I was given to understand was the emblem of the Monceux family; it had been affixed by hand while Marian shopped for the rest of the items on her list.

She had gold beading draped from the shoulders over antique white leather gloves, and a high mantle of white lace featuring rhinestones and crystals. She had on a rhinestone crown, too, and carried a scepter to go with. For all I knew, the rhinestones could have been vastly more costly and unfaux, but I wouldn't give the bitch the satisfaction. I was surprised not to see big, white plumes stuck into her hair, but it was evident that Maid Marian knew when to stop. I didn't know you could walk into a shop and walk out with such an outfit.

"Well," she goes, "what do you think?" She flounced a little and did this ganky turn on the floor, like I was supposed to be impressed or something.

"It's okay," I go, "but what would you wear that thing to?"

"Oh," she goes, "hospital openings and charity balls. We get invited to quite lot of that sort of thing. Do they have balls in the States?"

"Do they have *balls?* You just try us sometime. Seems like you did that twice in our history, and we sent you home both times, bitching and moaning about unfair tactics."

Maid Marian got a little ungelled by that statement, and she goes, "Talk about bitch!"

Robin Hood put his hand on her sleeve to cool her down. "Remember where she's from," he goes. "And you've clearly won the first round."

"Yeah," I go, "she did, but talk about unfair tactics!"

"Let's move on to the second challenge," goes Robin. "The normal, daily outfit. That shouldn't be too hard here, and I don't think we have much of an advantage."

"Fine. Back here at four o'clock. And no secret shops hidden behind some totally dis American cheesesteak shop."

"There was no secret about Whitley's," goes Maid Marian. "You could have shopped there, too. I could've gotten you a special guest entré."

"Oh, thank you very much, your serene highness. You look ridiculous. Go bless some war veterans or something."

We stormed off in opposite directions. Robin Hood looked as if he didn't really want to be a part of this contest anymore, and I couldn't blame him.

I headed back to Rhodes and Maxwell, because my fashion coordinator, whom I'd gotten to know as Miss Haye, had been so cordial. She seemed genuinely glad to see me, particularly now that I was wearing my woofin' blue fringy number and not the barbarian garb. "Yes?" she goes. "Something more?"

"I thought some simple but elegant afternoon wear, in case I meet a fresh young man with designs to take me to tea."

"Ah, yes, we have just the thing." This came off the rack, though, not out of one of the drawers. It was a peach wool cinch waist dress that I could see myself roaring to victory over Maid Marian in. The fashion coordinator threw in a chunky real gold necklace with matching earrings and a fun little floppy beret. She graciously suggested shoes and a handbag that were perfect mates.

I paid again for the costume, and this time she wrapped the extraneous faux-silk number and its accoutrements. I was sure that I looked at the top of my form, and I couldn't wait to see if Maid Marian had found anything better. Maybe there was another private shop somewhere that catered to local mythical types.

We both arrived at the teashop at four o'clock, and this time Robin Hood brought Little John to act as judge.

"Jeez, he's big!" I go.

"Whence the name," goes Robin Hood charmingly. I was definitely hittin', but Robin's girlfriend was a definite goober.

And goober she proved to be. She showed up in a kind of pink and yellow flowered sheath dress with a peplum. Her shoes were simple pink low-heeled walking shoes. Oh, and she had an ice lemon tote that looked as if it had been given to her as a gift from one of the overjoyed war veterans.

"Well," goes Robin Hood disappointedly.

"I award the imaginary golden arrow to Miss Birnbaum, making this contest a tie now," announced Little John. "The winner will be determined by the victor of the casual wear competition. Good luck to you both."

"Terrific!" I go. "Nobody can out-casual me."

"We'll see," goes Maid Marian, whisking off Robin Hood down one of the diagonal aisles.

"And we didn't choose a prize for the winner, did we?" I go. "How about picking up the tab for dinner."

"So damn Yank," goes Maid Marian over her shoulder. "Like the honor isn't enough for her."

I studied the mall's Where-to-Find map for a few minutes, until I saw an entry for a sporty, informal shop called The Box. It looked okay from the outside—no dry-skinned plain girls from Australia, no ethnically-mixed groups with outrageous accessories. I went into The Box and shopped around, and put together a nice assortment of informal clothes. The fashion coordinator was a young woman with pretty red hair and an obligatory green dress. She wore a nametag that said she was Caroline.

"Are you sure you're in the right shop, miss?" she goes. "You're wearing such a nice outfit—"

"Oh, don't worry, Caroline," I go. "I want to get out of this thing and into something more casual. I've picked these right off the racks. I think they'll be okay."

"A Yank, are we? And how are we enjoying our stay?"

"Just total it up," I go. I'd chosen a kind of artsy-radical ensemble that I thought would blow Miss S. Forest out of the water. I could see Paula Abdul wearing the outfit, but not Miss Princess Maid Marian.

"It ought to flatter you nicely," Caroline goes.

"Oh," I go, "I have this one-of-a-kind flair. I don't go overboard into artistic or anything. I just want to be comfortable."

"Oh," laughed Caroline, "anything would be comfortable after that costume. Shall I wrap it for you? Do you wish to wear your purchases out of the shop?"

"You bet I'll wear it," I go. "That was the whole idea." I paid Caroline and wished her a good day, and left wearing a black cotton knit jumpsuit with a baggy jacket and a wild, jungle-print belt. On my feet I had red loafers, and I didn't bother with a handbag—I kept all my little personal items in a bag from The Box. It was a pretty simple shopping expedition, and I knew I had Maid Marian beaten by the kilometer.

I arrived at the tea shop about half-past five. Robin and Marian were nowhere in sight, but Little John was inside having some British goodies unknown to us in the colonies. "Hey," he goes, "you look downright delicious! Maybe I shouldn't be the judge, because I'm quantifiably prejudiced toward exotic women."

"*I'm* exotic?" I go, like totally disbelieving, but loving every second of it.

"I like the jacket over the jumpsuit. Very Seventh Avenue. And that intensely sexy Yank accent!"

"You know Seventh Avenue?" I go. It seemed like we had a lot in common. And my New York nasal whine—*sexy?*

Robin Hood and Maid Marian took a lot longer to choose the casual clothing than any of the other outfits. I would've thought their traditional costumes would've been hot enough for show—you know, Robin's Lincoln green and Marian's dynamic retro old-timey gear; but I could tell that Marian wanted to absolutely kill here. So while Little John and I made goo-goo eyes over plates of like this terribly weight-inducing stuff, we waited but we didn't notice the time go by.

"So," I go, "I understand that you're this big superstar in the Video Arcade."

Little John blushed. "Aw," he goes, "has Gentle Robin been bragging on me again? It's just because he has no control over the silver ball. From the time he shoots it, he has maybe three seconds before it drops out one of the exit holes. He only plays those games because he doesn't like the video games where all you do is kill people."

"Except Normans, I suppose."

"Yes, well, killing Norman invaders, it goes without saying."

I stuffed some more pastry into my mouth. "Do you mind me asking a couple of embarrassing questions?"

"No, lady, I fear not," goes Little John.

"Well," I go, "take for instance Robin's name. Surely it's short for Robert, which is of Norman origin."

Little John frowned. "Causes him no end of grief, tackling that one."

"And if I remember right, the date of King Richard's return given in the book is something like 1188."

"Close enough," goes Little John, beginning to look grief-stricken himself.

"And you all escaped together to miss out on like the tyranny of the Normans. But the longbow—your band's chosen weapon—was not the favorite weapon of the Saxons, it was the short bow. The longbow wasn't even known by the Normans. It wasn't introduced until the end of the thirteenth century, at the battle of Falkirk. Am I right so far?"

"Have some more of this cream cake. It's pretty hittin', as far as mall food goes."

"No, thank you," I go.

"You seem to have studied up on us right well."

I shrugged. "It was either the Myths and Legends course or a political science thing I never would've gotten through."

"I know the feeling, the first time I saw Robin shoot—and it was a clothyard shaft from a longbow."

"Well," I go, "how do you explain your pardons from King Richard upon his return? In 1188 or thereabouts, the monarch, as far as I recall, was Henry II Plantagenet, not Richard."

A fainter shrug from Little John. "Prettier remembering than I have these days, my lady."

"And then there's your own name. John was introduced by the Normans, and at that time 'Little' meant in Saxon mean or like a lying, skanky son of a bitch."

Little John shrugged. "What can I say about what others thought of me at an early age?"

"Am I making you uncomfortable with all these questions?" I go.

Little John gave me a faint smile. "No," he goes, "I'll give as fair as I get, to the best of my recollection."

"Why do you put up with all this rumormongering?" I go.

"Oh," goes Little John, "it's only among the pedantic academics. Robin's gotten us a new PR firm, though. We'll be hot stuff again soon."

Robin and Marian entered the tea shop about 6 o'clock. They took empty seats at the table with Little John and me.

"Well," goes Maid Marian, "what do you think?" She stood and turned slowly, showing off her outfit. She had bought for herself a pair of Harris tweed pleated trousers, soft grey flecked with yellow, blue, and green. Above the pants she wore a beautiful, pale blue hand-knit sweater decorated with a pattern of colorful May flowers. Under the sweater she had on a leaf green turtleneck. On her feet she had grey woolen socks and sturdy black oxfords. She smiled delightedly at the assemblage and then took her seat. Robin stood up and he goes "There isn't any more of a casual outfit in England today than right here at this table." He slammed his ale tankard on the table and sat down.

"It will be very difficult," goes Little John, "for me to choose the final winner and award the cherished prize today."

"In that outfit, Marian," I go, "you look like the Queen of the May."

Marian glared at me. "I've been Queen of the May with Robin as King of the May for 700 years. In Nottinghamshire, no one would dare propose any others."

"Well, then, Little John," goes Robin Hood, "don't feel obliged to name us the winners just because we've been winners for over seven centuries. We have a worthy challenger among us. We'll think no less of you for championing Miss Birnbaum over us." Robin was one gracious dude.

"They're both pretty nice outfits," Little John goes. "I think we'll have to look in more detail to break this apparent tie."

Robin stood and finished another tankard of ale. "Never before in seven hundred years," he goes, "has a contest finished as closely as this. Of course, during the majority of those years Sherwood Forest was a forest, not a mall." He sat back down.

Little John got up and walked around to see me and Maid Marian better. First he examined me. I tried not to be ganky, and I kept a straight face, although I knew I was looking good. He made a circuit of our table two or three times, and each time he complimented me on my choices of casual clothes. "I've said it before, but I think you've got crushin' taste in clothes. I'm a sucker for fringe, but I won't let that get in the way of my judgment.

Maureen, you're what we've come to call in the last few years a real betty—that's totally good. I think your figure and your fitness add to your point total because here in Sherwood we expect a woman to be more than just a lovely lady at our service. Your outfit is outstanding. For instance, your belt. What about it?"

"Oh, it's nothing special," I go. "I picked it up for forty pounds. Hand made in Brazil. How much is that in dollars?"

"Very nice. Very nice. Now let's look at Marian's ensemble. Your pants are a lovely Harris tweed. And your sweater?"

"Hand knit of Scottish lambswool."

"And the turtleneck. A perfect spring green background for the flowers in your sweater."

Robin Hood ordered more ale for all of us, the first for Little John and me. Robin took a long draught and, burping, announced "Can Marian shop or can't she?" At which point, Little John rubbed his well-trimmed beard again and examined Maid Marian's clothes more carefully.

"You know," he goes, "I do honestly believe by the king's troth that I've seen that leaf green turtleneck before."

"No!" cried Robin Hood. Maid Marian's expression fell slowly into grief.

"Even after seven hundred years," she goes, "I cannot bear to win under falsehood. I have worn this green turtleneck before. Look, here on my sleeve, this hole. I received this shirt two years ago from my aunt—on the Monceux side. I knew it would look good with these other clothes, and I thought that I might easily dupe Little John who would be the hard judge and Maureen who is not accustomed to our ways. Forgive me! I have forfeited the match! I don't deserve your faith and trust any longer."

Little John's expression was grim. "You've served us in Sherwood Forest all these centuries in every necessary capacity. Surely you've earned our gratitude enough to overcome this one lapse in judgment."

"Thank you," goes Maid Marian simply.

Robin goes "Marian, I love you still, and I always will. Maureen, I'm happy to offer you membership in our Merrie Band. You're right hearty and we'd be pleased to have you as a member of our group."

And just then, with a rich cream pie in my mouth, I whooshed out of Merrie Olde England.

MAUREEN, LISTEN," I told her, "I'm not as enthusiastic about your adventures as you are. I've got my own life to lead. I'm married now, and pregnant. Although you'll be my best friend for life, probably, and we have our Greenberg School bond between us, I have to tell you that you've become a disruptive force in our family."

"Bitsy," she said, "I don't know how to tell you this, but I've had a really bald time here. I understand from my careful observational studies that Mars is in the sky tonight, and I'll make another attempt to whoosh to the Red Planet and Prince Van. I'm beginning to lose hope that I'll ever find him again, but I have to keep trying. The first time was biscuit easy. Since then, I've been lucky just to make it back to Earth. I wonder if any of the scientists at the Smithsonian Institute or those burly places in England could help me out.

"But if you truly feel this way about me, I wish you all the luck in the world with your husband and your coming child and I suppose I'll leave you alone from now on."

I watched her walk dejectedly out of my house, then slowly she turned on the steps and she said "We'll always be as good friends as are Robin, Little John, and Marian."

She looked up into the sky and saw that dusk was already falling; it was no problem to pick out the red planet of Mars, and she whooshed off on one last try to corner the terribly unattainable Prince Van.

The editorial team of Richard Gilliam and Ed Kramer put together an anthology of stories about the Holy Grail, and they specifically requested a Maureen Birnbaum tale to lighten the mix. I learned very quickly that it's sometimes pretty tough to write funny stories on Certain Subjects.

Maureen Birnbaum
and the Saint Graal

Maureen Birnbaum
and the Saint Graal

by Elizabeth Spiegelman-Fein

(as told to George Alec Effinger)

WHAT CAN *I tell you? The last time Maureen Birnbaum zetzed into my life, I was 5/9ths pregnant with our darling little Malachi Bret. My husband, Josh, never got along with Muffy, and so he wasn't like terribly broken-hearted when she said she was probably never going to bother us again.*

Me, on the other hand, I was glad at first and then like I started to miss her. Not that I missed the gold brassiere and G-string she wore on her interplanetary jaunts, or the way huge broadsword named Old Betsy (no relation) she dragged with her into my nice clean Queens apartment. And not that I missed her endless braggy narrations of her really, really hard-to-believe exploits. What I missed, I'm thinking, is our old Greenberg School friendship, which belongs in the dim, dark past. What I missed was my evaporating youth.

See, Muffy still looks like a high school junior, and who wouldn't hate her on account of a thing like that? I, on the same other hand mentioned above, have become a little old housewife lady. I'll be thirty years old before I even get to the next paragraph. That was probably an exaggeration.

Okay. It was a rainy summer day and I'd dropped Malachi Bret off with

99

Mums so I could like do some personal time gazing wistfully at crushin', killer leather shoes that'd probably fit, too, but I couldn't buy them because now I'm a militant vegetarian after reading Sidney Sheldon's remake of Sinclair Lewis's immortal novel, The Jungle.

I was driving into the city in the maroon Renault Alliance Josh bought me (used, although he's a doctor with a healthy practice and like he could certainly have gotten me a better car and I don't see why not a new one) after the little Mazda died. I was halfway across the bridge when I heard this sort of fwumping sound and felt a gust of wind inside my car. Like I'm sure if the windows hadn't been rolled down, they'd've blown right out. I almost lost control of the steering wheel, and then I heard her.

"Whoa nelly, sister! Get a grip!"

It was guess what Muffy.

Oh, and by the way, I didn't mean Sinclair Lewis before, I'm so sure (now, I mean). It was Upton Sinclair! Is my face red! I always get them mixed up.

Like anyway, I shoot Muffy a quick glance and I was shocked. I mean I was almost never shocked by the weirdo outfits she showed up in, but this one was a weensy bit over the top. She was wearing a tight white dress hiked halfway up her chubby thighs, and it was made out of—I knew it right off—honest to God samite. *I don't even know how I knew, but I did. I mean, I'd never seen samite before, like it's not something they sell by the yard at Korvettes' or anything.*

So she goes, "Miss me, Bits?" Now it was "Bits." It made me long for the good old Bitsy days.

I just turned back to her and stared for a couple of seconds to establish the mood. Then I go, "Can I drop you somewhere, Muffs?"

Now like I really wish I had.

LOOK, I'M TELLING YOU, Bitsy, Fate can be cruel. Cruel to a heart that's true. How I've yearned—and like it's no big secret, right? because I keep telling you and I'm not even sure you believe me anymore—O, how I've yearned to whoosh back to Mars! Mars the red! Mars the terrible! Mars the bloody! Mars the home of the totally awright Prince Van, the buffest, tuffest babe in all of dudedom! Yet what does the universe do to me? It schleps me to Sherwood Forest—and a Sherwood Forest like spotlessly *sans* Kevin Costner, no less—and then schleps me to your house, then schleps me to God—and I do mean

God—knows where, then schleps me like *I don't believe this* not to your house, but to your terminally skanky *car*. Forgive me, Bits, but like it's skanky and I'm so sure you know it.

Where was I? Like don't ask me. I aimed like I always do for Mars, and like I always do I missed. Not my fault, I was carrying a lot of weight what with Old Betsy and the rest of the accoutrements I've gathered in my world-saving travels. Maybe like I forgot to allow for windage or something. Whatever. I opened my eyes and saw that I was definitely not on Mars. It's getting to be easier for me to identify *not on Mars.* It's a gravity and blue sky thing. Yeah, huh.

There was a road. There's always a goddamn road, even in the center of the Earth or wherever. So I stood in the road and nothing was happening and nothing was happening, so finally it dawns on me that this time I had to like walk.

So I hefted Old Betsy across my shoulder and marched onward into adventure like any sun-bronzed warrior woman would do. I was like unafraid and ready to turn the tables on the evildoers. Just like roads, there's always evildoers, know what I mean?

So I'm bookin' it along this dirt lane, and I'm watching the sun. It's going up. Then it's like noon, you know? and then it's going down. I'm still walking. I haven't seen anybody or anything, not a cow, not a field, not a castle on a hill, not anything. Of course, being a fierce fighting woman, I'm not like dismayed or nothing about having to spend the night in the shelter-ing roots of a primeval oak tree, because although some male-dominated mythologies have this cockamamy idea that oaks are dudelike in their tree-ness, oaks have historically been shown to be the temples-houses of druid-esses, from which we get the word, what is it? druades or something. And if the tree nymphets could live in an oak, I didn't mind sleeping with one. Sisterhood is, you know, like powerful and all.

I was just about to wrap myself in my combat cloak, if I'd had a combat cloak (and while I'm wishing, I could have used a down-filled vest from L. L. Bean, too) when what should happen but a gnarly old man (and I *do not* mean that in any good surfer-dudelike way) hobbles into view along the dusty road. Figures, huh?

Oh, my *gawd,* I go, it's like the first person I see and already I have a moral dilemma. See, that's how the Goddess tests you, like she keeps scat-tering moral dilemmas around like carpet tacks. It's much more obvious to a heroine like myself, but I'll bet even you, Bits, has to make R & I decisions now and then, for sure, huh? That's "radical and intense," honey, don't give me that look.

Here were my choices: I could curl up prettily and hit the rack, or I could like introduce myself politely to the raggedy dude and find out where the hell I was *this* time. No, you don't have to worry, Bits, like they always speak English. Another function of the universe, I guess, and I see no need to overtax my splendid brain worrying about it.

It was a real poser, let me tell you. I held a secret ballot, and interviewing the venerable old gentleman dude won over flaking out by a tally of six to four. So I put on my medium-power smile, the one that goes "I bear you no ill will but I'll slice you like a radish if I catch so much as an evil flicker in your eyes."

"My good man," I go, stepping into the road and gazing levelly at him. Gazing levelly is like a vital fighting person kind of trait. Some of us are born with it, huh.

"Good my lady," he goes. "What would you of me?"

And I'm like, whoa, funny English again. I just knew I was in some grody prehistoric time before people discovered the truth and traded in their Louis Vuitton handbags for Fendi.

"I would of you like your name, for openers," I go.

"Hight I merely Joe," he goes.

"Joe." A guy named Joe, and he's going around woulding and highting." And je suis Maureen Birnbaum, bravery like personified, and don't you ever, *ever* call me Muffy. I left that part of me long ago and, you know, far away."

Joe nodded thoughtfully, then gave me one of those shrewd, calculating looks, you know, where you feel like your thoughts are, oh, laid bare and lying there etherized upon the table like when old Miss Grau tried to make us understand "Prufrock," remember? Talk about a pair of scuttling claws. Jeez.

Well, now that you ask, Bits, I truly don't know *what* that has to do with my awesome adventure. It was an image, that's all. No biggie. Like forget it if it's too deep for you.

So he's like, "Wittest thou what I wot?"

Just the latest in un-key, dear. And they don't sell like Cliff Notes for real life, huh. I go, "No, I wit not."

"Wot I that thou art in the way of the Saint Graal."

I looked around quick, but nothing was coming. The wrinkly grandpop was operating on E. C. T. Estimated Cloud Time. I wasn't in anybody's way, for sure. "Well," I go, "in that case I'll just be moseying."

"None but the gentlest and most parfait knight may hope to achieve that goal."

Gentle, I'm thinking, hey, I could be gentle if I had a reason. Parfait, though, would take some thought. Hot fudge, definitely. Whipped cream, definitely. Six or seven maraschino cherries, most definitely. Ice cream? A tough choice, but I leaned toward mint chocolate chip and a scoop of bubble gum. "I think I can hack it," I go.

Joe give me this little smile like "Yeah, we'll see." I wot like instantly that I might have to watch myself around this guy. "Wouldst thou then accompany me?"

"I dunno," I go. "Maybe *you* could accompany *me*." I was like there first, you know? It probably doesn't seem important to you, Bits, but billing is heavy stuff to a brawny warrior. Image is like everything, and you got to let people know from the getgo that they can't dis you without immediate and terrible retribution.

"As thou wishest," he goes.

So we walk maybe a half mile, neither of us saying much of anything. It's getting dusky and dark and stars are coming out and I look for Mars in the sky but the strife-torn God of War was like totally absent. When I look down again, what to my wondering eyes should appear but *another* shabby dude in a filthy robe and hood. He looked like the Hermit in the Tarot deck if the Hermit had gone residentially challenged—that's, come on you know, like homeless—for a year or so. Definitely not Block Island Race Week, Bits.

"Hola!" I go, but like soft.

"Behold, it is my brother Bohort."

Honest to goodness, honey, I could've sworn he said the most insulting thing. He didn't, though, I found out. "Your brother," I go warily. "What a whatchacall, a coincidence."

Gives me him that same dumb smile, all sort of bemused and condescending. "Not that we are twins of the womb, but yet are we brothers in Christ."

"Christ," I go. "Well, yeah, huh."

"Bohort!" he goes. "Well met!"

"God's grace to you, brother Joseph!" goes Bohort.

"And to you, good man. Behold Maureen, a lady knight errant who seeketh that which we wot of."

"Ah," goes his friend, "then gladly will we share our company."

"Fine," I go sternly, "but you can drop the 'lady knight' business. I'm a knight, period. None of this setting me off in a special category just on account of my gender."

Joe looked at Bohort, and Bohort looked at Joe. "Shall we continue on toward the Castle of Seemly Joy, or take our rest?" goes Joe. I'll like stop reporting their weird antique English if you don't mind, Bits.

Well, again the vote went for moving on, and so like we did. Okay. Now it's nighttime and we're still marching along. For once I didn't have to worry about where I was going, although like I didn't know what to expect from the Castle of Seemly Joy when I got there. The name of the place sounded like, you know, a massage parlor or something.

So I was lost in thought, something I try to do every few days—a healthy mind in a tuff bod, n'est-ce pas? I wasn't paying much attention to the scenery until I noticed that we'd come to a fork in the road. "Aiee," I go, "a fork in the road."

"Even so," goes Joe. "A leftward turning and in like wise a rightward turning. Whichsoever shall we choose?"

"Don't look at *me*," I go. "I mean, I'm following you guys, like for sure."

"Then we ask you to choose," goes Bohort.

"I know," I go. "I'll choose the fork that takes us to . . . the Castle of Seemly Joy."

"Excellent brave choice!" goes Joe in an exclamatory kind of way.

"Uh huh. Now which road is it?"

"Alas, we cannot tell you," goes Bohort. "The way differs for every pilgrim."

"Pilgrim?" I go. "Do I *look* like a pilgrim? What is this, a Thanksgiving pageant or something? Last time I looked, it wasn't even the Fourth of July."

"Choose," goes Joe.

And I'm like, "What the hell? This castle moves around over the countryside or something?"

Joe and Bohort looked at each other. They didn't say a word.

"We'll go to the right," I tell them.

"How now," goes Bohort. Don't ask *me*, Bitsy.

So we hike it off to the right, and lo and behold not a quarter of a mile further on we come to a knight in full armor on horseback with a couched lance, just sort of idly sitting in the road waiting hour after hour after hour for us to come by. Like some people don't have anything better to do with their lives.

"What ho, varlets," goes the knight. He had a big shield with black stripes that divided the shield into three parts, like a peace symbol without the middle leg thingy. In the upper left section was sort of a pig with tusks all rampanty. In the upper right section were three red shapes like Lego blocks. In the bottom section was a gold-colored crown with bright enameled jewels. And like not a ding on that shield, like he just bought it that morning and nobody had bonked it yet.

"Who you calling varlets?" I go, stepping to the fore, see, 'cause I was like the only one in our group with courageous battle-hardened nerves.

"Y'all I'm calling varlets," goes Sir Fruit Loop.

"Why don't you get off that horse and try it?" I go.

"Try what?" he goes.

"Try this." I waved Old Betsy around a couple of times. I had a feeling that inside his tin helmet, this guy was no rocket scientist.

He didn't say anything. He set his lance upright in some kind of socket thing, swung his leg heavily over the saddle, and landed with a noisy clanging on the ground beside his horse. Then he drew his own broadsword and came at me slowly. He moved sort of like Robbie the Robot, you know, huh? Clanking and shuffling. I figured he had one good swing with that sword of his, and if I kept out of its way, I had maybe fifteen minutes to dice him up while he recovered for the next swipe.

"Ware the knight," goes Joe. "He is the first Guardian of the Pearly Path, and your first Test."

I glanced over my shoulder. "You didn't say anything about tests. I would've taken this adventure pass/fail if I'd had a choice."

"Good my lady," goes Bohort, "you made that choice when you took the rightwise turning."

"Uh huh," I go, watching my opponent awkwardly hoisting his sword for the first strike. "And like what would we have met on the leftwise way?"

"Alackaday, the selfsame Guardian."

I would've put down money that he was going to say that.

Like I'm turning my attention back to the lethal threat in front of me. "Who are you?" I go.

"I am Sir Sanspeur," he goes.

"And you've got a brother named Sansreproche or something a little further on, don't you?" I am like so clever sometimes, Bits, I amaze myself.

By way of reply, this Sanspeur dude tried to whang me a good one on top of my head. If that blow had landed, I'd be sitting here dead, split from my skull straight down to my highly-prized groinal area.

But you'll be happy to learn the blow didn't land. I neatly side-stepped—I mean, I had all the time in the world, like you know?—and while he was trying to unstick his blade from the ground, I just gave him a little sideways whack with Old Betsy, not hurting him much but sending his own sword flying away.

"O, I am undone," Sanspeur goes in a quavery voice. "You have bested me, and you are therefore a most terrible strong Maid."

"I'm nobody's maid, buster," I go fiercely. "Now, do we get to pass by you without any of your nonsense?"

For answer, Sir Sanspeur merely hung his ironclad head. I didn't even look behind me to catch Joe and Bohort's reactions. I kind of relished the moment of victory, which I knew wasn't going to last very long, because whenever there's a first Test, you can bet your Bernardo sandals there'll be another.

So I'm like, "What is this Saint Graal when it's at home?"

And Joe goes, "Saint Graal is Frankish for Holy Grail."

"Ah," I go, "The Holy Grail. You mean the Sacred Cauldron."

Joe looked at Bohort, and Bohort looked at Joe. "I don't believe I've ever heard the Grail called that," goes Bohort.

"Not surprising," I go, stifling an imaginary yawn. "Holy Grail is a male-supremacist sexist revisionist term using religion to hide the devious conspiracy to rob women of their innate power and authority granted to them by the Goddess."

"Goddess?" goes Joe. I thought he was going to strangle on the word.

"Don't pretend you don't know what I'm talking about," I go.

Well, they did so pretend. Bohort goes, "Of course, the Saint Graal or Sangreal, the Holy Grail as you would have it, is the chalice used by Jesus at the Last Supper. Its history is long and magical. It was fashioned from a gigantic jewel, a gem that had once been part of a magnificent crown given by sixty thousand angels to Lucifer, when that archangel still dwelt in Heaven. During his fall into Hell, the jewel fell from his crown to Earth, where it was fashioned into a cup. The cup came at last into the possession of a certain good man, who gave it to Jesus."

"Nuh uh, that's not the way the secret traditions of women have it," I go.

"What secret traditions?" goes Joe. I thought I saw a flicker of fear in his eyes.

"The chalice is actually the Sacred Cauldron, the symbol of women tri-

106

umphant, the symbol of female power, as the cross is the symbol of male power."

Bohort looked horrified. "How can you claim the Holy Grail is a feminine symbol?"

And I'm like, "Isn't it a treasure that all men seek?"

Joe goes, "Wellll, yes."

"There's more," I go. I was getting into this. I don't know if I got all my facts straight, though, 'cause like I was trying to remember what I learned from Miss Stickney in sophomore Women's Studies. "The Three Sisters are the counterparts of your divine Trinity. They show up everywhere: The Triple Goddess, the Norns, the three Graces, the three witches in *MacBeth*, the three cauldrons of Wise Blood that Odin stole, there's no end to it."

There was silence for a while. Finally Bohort spoke up. "It doesn't make any difference, anyway," he said. "Sir Galahad achieved the Saint Graal because he was the only knight of the Round Table who was still a maiden."

"Galahad?" I go. "Like a virgin?"

"Certes," goes Joe. "Only a person untainted by profane love may long to see such a holy relic."

"Well," I go, drawing myself up to my full height, which is impressive to these short little ancestors of ours. "I myself am a maiden and about as taintless as you can get. But if you tell anybody—*anybody*—I'll damn well tear your lips off." I had been meaning to lose my virginity, Bits, but I'd been busy, first with you know school and all, then with hacking apart green Martians and God knows what. Now it looked like hooray being a virgin was going to get me somewhere.

"As my brother said," goes Joe, "Sir Galahad achieved the Saint Graal, following which it was removed unto Heaven forever. Now and then someone like Lancelot will have a vision of it, but not physical contact."

"And who knows from visions?" I go. "Jeez, I've had some visions—"

"So in these latter days the Queste has another goal," goes Bohort.

I felt my eyes narrowing like suspiciously. "And what may that be?"

"The Saint Nappie," goes Bohort. "The berry bowl used by Jesus at the Last Supper."

"Berry bowl?" I go. See, I was like fabulously dubious. "I don't remember berries at the Last Supper. I mean, if they'd had berries, they'd be part of the Catholic mass now, wouldn't they? Between the bread and wine?"

"I suppose," goes Bohort. "But I didn't say they had berries. I said they had a six-inch bowl. It is part of the Mystery what the bowl contained."

"Could've been rose water," goes Joe.

"Could've been Judas's petty cash bowl," I go.

Silence again.

"And the Saint Nappie?" I go.

"It is lodged on Earth, man wot not where. Perhaps it rests within the Castle of Seemly Joy, awaiting those who may find that holy shrine," goes Bohort.

I glanced from one to the other, a determined look on my face and the light of true conviction in my eyes. "Follow me, men!" I cried. I felt kind of like Gregory Peck in *Pork Chop Hill*. Ever since I first whooshed my way to Mars, I've known that I was born to command—and like not only command, but I was born to rule. I saw myself as a female Odysseus, wandering hither and yon in search of my own true love, fighting the worst battles against overwhelming odds and emerging all, you know, triumphant and stuff. Then someday I'd go found my own city and rule it benevolently until it was time for me to disappear magically and then there'd be all these like too strenuous to believe myths about where I was buried and how I was just waiting to return whenever my realm needed me no matter how many centuries had passed. See, I did too read that Joseph Campbell stuff. And I thought it was pretty dumb. I mean, don't you wonder what his wife thought about it all, huh?

Anyway. I had the feeling that there was something ho daddy weird happening around me because we'd been like making tracks for hours and I'd already been involved in one deadly combat, and I was still wide awake, I wasn't tired or hungry or thirsty, I didn't even have to pee. And jeez, Bits, you know my bladder's about the size of a walnut. So I had the feeling that I was caught up in some eldritch mystical Queste, on account of you never hear of like Sir Perceval having to stop and pee.

The trees—heavy oak action all around—arched over us like a green tunnel. It was shadowy and quiet—*too* quiet, like just before one of the camp counselors gets his head cut off by a chainsaw in a *Friday the 13th* movie. There was, as Mr. Stumpf would say, Gloomigkeit all over the place. Of course, I was concerned only for my fellow travelers, who did not have my strict and noble warrior woman code of behavior to fall back on. Yeah, huh.

Okay, like the road turned sharply to the right, and when we rounded the bend, there was this like rock right in the middle of our path. "Gladsome tidings!" goes Bohort. Like he was *such* an enthusiastic dude I wanted to slap him silly sometimes.

"Pardonnez moi," I go, "but what is so gladsome about a boulder in the road?"

"Why, good my lady," goes Joe, "mark you not it is a magic boulder?"

"I mark nothing, pal," I go. "All I see is something that would rip the bottom out of any wagon wants to come by this place. And if that rock has been sitting here all this time without somebody digging it up and heaving it off to the side, I think probably no wagon ever did come by here. That leaves me with like one question: Then what is this road for, if nobody ever comes by here?"

"It is a magic stone, forsooth, and a magic road," Bohort took pleasure in assuring me.

"A magic stone. I spieth nothing in the way of an enchanted sword sticking out of it. Or am I too late for that?"

Bohort and Joe thought that was somewhat amusing and uttered like several ha ha's each. Then Joe goes, "Look thou not upon the stone, yet verily beneath it."

"Under the stone," I go. "Lemme see if I got this straight. There's something really neat under this stone. Like worms, maybe. Or Japanese beetles. Or a trapdoor into a vast and eerie subterranean wonderland of fabulous riches and you know nightmarish Lovecraftian gel-creatures."

Bohort looked at Joe, and Joe looked at Bohort. They were smiling, but answer came there none.

I grumbled a little and hoofed it over to the boulder. I did my rally best, putting my mighty thews to work rocking the stone. I prayed to the Goddess, or any one-third of her that might be listening, for sufficient strength, but it was like N. G. No go, Bits, at least. I can think of two or three other things N. G. could stand for, how come you can't? You should watch "Wheel of Fortune" every once in a while, that's what you should do, huh.

Well, it was like plenty clear that I wasn't going to roll that rock out of the road. I thought about the problem for a while. Then—in the famous words of my role model, Wonder Woman, "Praise Hera!"—I had a sudden insight, you know? Ever happen to you, Bitsy? A sudden insight? No, I thought not. So what I did was, I used my multi-talented sword as a simple machine—no, not a pendulum. A lever. Wasn't it Einstein who said, "Give me a lever and a house in the country and I can move the world?" Or something like that. What do you mean, "fulcrum?" I'll use your head for a fulcrum, you don't let me finish my saga.

Well, to make a long story come to an end, I clean and jerked that boulder out of the dirt. Then I bent way down to see what Bohort and Joe had been talking about. It was a dirty number-ten window envelope with a sheet of paper inside. I took the paper out and read it. It said:

> Hello, pilgrim!
> Welcome to Clue #1! You've evidently surmounted the great difficulties put in your way, and you are to be congratulated! Now, if you keep up your courage (and stay pure! Pure is the way to go, whatever your disgusting fleshly senses may counsel you) you will soon acquire that which you heartily desire! So here it is, the first important clue!
> *The Saint Nappie rests on a deep blue satin pillow in the Great Hall of the Castle of Seemly Joy.*
> All best, and may God bless!

I crumpled the sheet of paper and the envelope into a ball and tucked them away in my utility pouch. A true barbarian swordsperson may revel in slaughter and all that kind of thing, but one does not litter the forest-ho.

"Now what?" I go.

"Onward!" cried Bohort. "Onward to the Castle of Seemly Joy!"

"What about the boulder?" I go.

"Oh," Joe goes in what you call your offhand manner, "someone will be by to reset it."

"With a new clue underneath?"

Joe looked at Bohort. "If that is the Lord's will," goes Bohort.

"Uh huh, you bet," I go. "The Goddess wouldn't have any part of this nonsense."

Before we'd traveled much further, Joe put his hand on my arm. "Forgive me, good my lady. I have a garment which will profit you much to don. It will mark you well as a holy pilgrim, and you will receive therefore the aid and succor of our allies."

He held out to me the very white schmatte in which I am even now encladded. I didn't think much of it at the time. I mean, *no designer label at all,* even on the *inside!* These two guys had never heard of the Talbots catalog. They probably never even heard of *Lane Bryant,* for God's sake!

So I took the raiment and garbed myself behind a set of bushes. I just like threw it on over my primitive but serviceable Ruler of the Everywhere gold bra and G-string. The white dress fit okay except it was snug across the you know *ass,* if we can speak freely. I would've liked to dab on a little Chanel #22—did I tell you I've moved up to Chanel now? Seems like I've never run into a single other warrior who wore *Je Reviens*. Not that I just follow the crowd or anything, Bits, but like who wants to be T. B. A. just because you smell wrong.

To Be Avoided, dear. Are you putting on fat between your ears, Bitsy? We used that one at Greenberg.

I'll be goddamned if I can remember what I was about to tell you. Maybe we can stop along here somewhere and have just the smallest little Bloody Mary? They're like just so *good* for you, too, you know, with all the vegetables and stuff. No? Too early? Ha, Bits, I think you'd positively freak if you saw how we savage fighters consume food and liquor shamelessly, in a free-flowing celebration of life and victory and not being pinned to the ground by a very sharp pointed thing.

Lemme see. Oh, yeah, like in another fifteen minutes or so we came to a falling down stone building. It looked like someplace the Vandals had lunch on their way to sack Rome, and they enjoyed the hospitality so much they made a point of trashing the place again on the way home. I looked at Joe and Bohort, and put forth the postulate that this, then, was the Castle of Seemly Joy, famed in song and legend.

They really shot me down, huh. "No, fair maiden," goes Bohort, "not so easily wilt thou arrive at that precious goal. This that thou beholdest is the Gladsome Abbey."

"Yeah, duh," I go. "It doesn't look so gladsome to me."

Joe shrugged. "There were more wonderful days, all long since," he goes. And like even if he didn't wink, he was implying it for all he was worth. I had to tread carefully here, Bits, 'cause I could sense Metaphorical Significance all over the place.

We went into the abbey, and boy howdy was I surprised that there wasn't any knightly dude in full battle array trying to stop us. There wasn't much of anybody, really. It looked worse on the inside: crumbling stone and fallen blocks, caved-in ceilings and shredded tapestries, scuffed and warped planking on the floor, rats scurrying around, and best of all nothing but moonlight to keep the orcs away.

We poked into one chamber after another and didn't see hide nor hair of any human residents. After we'd gone through ten or twelve rooms, I found a suspicious pool of light in one corner. I turned around and saw that a silver beam of moonlight glimmered through a chink high up on the wall. I could hardly believe our luck, that the moon just happened to be in position to illuminate the very corner that like just happened to also be indicated by a big, wide, bright red arrow painted about knee-high on an adjacent wall.

"How fortunate," goes Joe.

"Really," I go. "How about that."

"What do you think it means?" Bohort goes.

I just squinched my eyes shut in like, you know, mock pain. I didn't bother to answer him. Instead, I got fully into hacking away at the dry-rotted floor boards with Old Betsy. In like a few minutes, I'd biffed open a hole big enough to put my hand into, so I put my hand into it. What should I find but a small leather pouch with a drawstring cord! How thrilling, huh?

Joe goes, "I wot not what mayest in the bag be." Joe wot not a lot of things.

"Perhaps we'll find out," I go, giving them like this little up-on-Mount-Olympus sneer. I pulled the bag open, and inside was a golden key, wrapped in a piece of paper. The problem was that mice or whatnot had gotten to the bag and the paper long before I had. Now the paper said:

—key.
        —may use it—
Good—   —bless.

"What is it?" goes Joe.

I looked fully at him and did not blink. "It's a key, Joe," I go. "It's probably Clue #2. Maybe it unlocks something here in the abbey."

"Well, no," goes Bohort.

"How do you know that?" I go.

Bohort looked like a guy who had sent in his subscription money to *Penthouse* and started getting *Architectural Digest* by mistake. "It just doesn't look like it would, that's all," he goes. Pretty lame, huh?

So we bailed out of the abbey on account of I figured Bohort probably knew what he was talking about, even though he was just ever so grieved that he'd let it slip. We hit the Pearly Path again until we smacked up against the second Test.

It was a big hairy serpent. Oh my *gawd*, Bitsy, no, the snake didn't have like *fur* or anything. It was hairy. *Hairy.* It's slang, Bits. Oh, just figure it out. So anyway I go to work on the serpent, all the time fully realizing that this was a thinly disguised phallic threat to my maiden-hoodedness. Like the serpent in the Garden of Eden, huh? No big surprise that Eve was

112

tempted by a big old charming male member, and like the mother of us all *just couldn't resist.* Of course, Bitsy, men wrote that book.

So I like lop the head of the snake and *by golly* two more grew back. I wasn't fighting a monster, I was fighting a literary illusion. I didn't have to lop any more heads to test my working hypothesis, so I went after the other end. I biffed off the snake's scaly tail, maybe eleven inches, enough for a whole 'nother meal if you'd wrap it in tin foil and put it in the freezer. Well, the snake didn't grow his tail back, so I whanged another chunk of tail, and then another and another. I kept slicing that two-headed son of a bitch until I had completed tail and was clearly into neck. The heads turned to watch what I was doing, and they were most evidently worried.

Finally, all I had left was this little V-shaped bit of monster, the two heads joined to maybe three inches of body. The heads just lay on the ground panting and looking pitiful. I left them like that, and we continued on our way.

"Excellent slicemanship!" Bohort goes. "You know that in my youth I myself carried a sword in the service of my king—"

"Arthur, would that be by any chance?" I go.

"—yes, King Arthur," goes Bohort. "And I was a stalwart of his Table. But never in all my days have I seen a soul so skillful with a blade. Except Lancelot, of course. And Perceval and Galahad, too. And Gawain and—"

"Yeah, huh," I go. "That was the second Test. How many are there altogether?"

"Now, that too differs with every pilgrim," goes Joe. "Most usually there are three, however."

"One more test and one more clue, right?" I go. "Things in threes?"

"Things in threes," goes Bohort. "Mirroring the holy and glorious Trinity."

"The Triple Goddess," I go. I watched them shiver. It was like good for them now and then.

Jeez-o-man, Bitsy, I could tell that I was getting close to the end of this exploit. I've got a sixth sense for knowing that by now. No, it's *not* women's intuition. Women's intuition is a male sexist demeaning fraudulent counter-revolutionary concept invented to put a name on something men can't ever understand because of their stunted and wholly unromantic natures. If you buy into the intuition thing you might as well climb back on that pedestal they set up to trap your ass.

What do you *mean*, Bitsy, you *like* being on a pedestal? Hell, next time I come back from some mind-shattering adventure, I'll bring some of my pamphlets with me. God, honey, you need a little consciousness-raising. And a fanny tuck wouldn't hurt you, either, if I may make a personal observation just between close friends.

Just never mind, okay? Just drop it, Bitsy, I'm coming to the gut-wrenching finale here. See, even though I guessed not more than two or three hours had passed, I noticed the sun trying to peep up over horizon. "What time is it?" I go.

"Dawn," goes Bohort. He was like ever so helpful.

I shrugged. If I could accept two-headed dreadful serpents, I could accept three-hour nights. Maybe I was in some warm polar region or something. It didn't make any difference. I didn't have much time to like ponder, on account of there was a giant blocking our way on the Pearly Path. A *big* giant, Bitsy, resting his elbow on the crown of a mighty oak tree.

"The third Test?" I go.

"The third Test," goes Joe.

I chewed my lip for a few seconds. It looked like the giant was ready to give me all the time in the world. "Say," I go finally, "where are all those allies you mentioned? I mean, that's why I'm dragging around in this white outfit, huh?" A magical white outfit, too, Bits, 'cause it never got dirty and serpent blood came clean with just a damp cloth.

"Why, we are those selfsame allies!" goes Bohort.

"Yeah, duh," I go. They still looked like two fully rasped-out fugitives from the dumpster behind Ernest and Julio Gallo's place.

"Behold!" goes Joe. And right there he whipped off his hooded robe, and doggone if underneath it he was wearing a tunic and like pants made out of the same white threads I was wearing. Only he had a red cross on his chest. And suddenly he didn't look anywhere as old and unshaven as he had when I first met him. He was now a young blond guy with twinkling eyes and apple cheeks.

Don't you just hate apple cheeks, Bitsy? You can never trust a guy with apple cheeks, no matter how mythological he is.

And Bohort did the same, flanging away his shredded robe. The two dudes looked like brothers, all right. "Know you not our tales?" goes Bohort.

"Nuh uh." I knew I was going to hear 'em, though. I glanced up at the giant, and he smiled at me. He was still in no particular rush.

"I am Joseph of Arimathea," goes Joe, "into whose keeping passed the Saint Graal, that I provided unto our Lord and Savior, and thencefrom

114

carried it I unto the nations of Britain, in order that it should be made ready for the beginning of the noblest of all Questes."

"Wow," I go.

"And I was the companion of Sir Perceval," goes Bohort, "and we had the greatest and surpassing honor to be with Sir Galahad upon the moment of the completion of his Queste. We beheld the most puissant Saint Graal, and we beheld Sir Galahad's most holy and peaceful death, and the angels that bare his soul unto Heaven."

And I'm like, "Wow," again. "So the two of you are going to pitch in and help me with this tall dude?"

"No," goes Joseph of Arimathea, "we'll watch. This is your third and final Test, and we mayest not help thee."

"Really," I go. Now, of course giants are just another phallic symbol, so I wasn't totally haired out or anything. I just fell back on Mrs. Stickney's feminist disclosures. According to Hindu traditions, giants could live a thousand years because like their whole existence was what they called centered in the blood. And the blood, you should forgive me, Bitsy, was the menstrual blood of the Triple Goddess. Oh, don't go *ewww*. This is all true stuff. You know of course that in Greek mythology, the River Styx was really a river of blood. Guess whose?

Look, I can't tell you where it says that. I just *know* it, that's all.

So I like pointed all this out to the giant, and he mulled it over for a while, a heavy frown on his craggy features. At last he came to some decision, because he just stepped out of my way. I guess I dazzled him with my brilliance or something. Anyway, I thanked him kindly and started again on my Queste.

"A moment, good my lady," goes Joe. "Wot ye not that the giant is to be slain?"

"What for?" I go. "Seems to me I was just supposed to get by him, and I done did that."

Joe looked at Bohort, and Bohort looked at Joe. "The giant is supposed to be dead," goes Bohort.

I shrugged. "A dead giant is a useless giant, and this giant looks pretty useless to me, so he might as well be dead. Come on if you're coming."

They hesitated a few seconds, and then they followed me, all right. I have these sterling leadership qualities, you know.

Clue #3 wasn't far away. It was just a note tacked to the last tree before a vast and peaceful meadow. The note said:

Seek thou, O fortunate pilgrim, seek thou the Castle of
Seemly Joy in thine heart of hearts.

Good luck, and may God bless.

"In my heart of hearts," I go. What was I supposed to do, tap my heels
together three times and wish? I had to think about this one. It wasn't, you
know, like the most revelatory clue in the world.

"The Castle of Seemly Joy," I go. "Joy, huh? As in Joyous Gard? Where
Guinevere split with Lancelot? You know that's just another name for
Venusberg which is another name for Mons Veneris. I don't have to spell
that one out, do I? See, like I said, it's all sexual symbols, but the male-
dominated terrified pathetic heterophobic Church co-opted them and
changed them into castrated and powerless images. But we women know.
We've been keeping notes."

"I wish you wouldn't say castrated," goes Bohort.

"Never mind," I go. "I know where the Castle is. 'Seemly Joy,' my heroic
ass. You *wish* it was Seemly. In your next life, dudes."

"Why . . . what do you mean?" goes Joe. He was turning into a real
hairball right before my eyes. I mean, Bitsy, he was getting into F. D. F. M.
N., you know? I don't *expect* you to get that one, sweetie, I just made it up.
Feet Don't Fail Me Now. He was like freaked, huh.

"What I mean is the Castle is right . . . over . . . there!" And I spun
to my left and pointed into the butterfly and songbird-filled meadow.

"Where?" goes Bohort. "I see nothing."

"There," I go, and sure enough, there was the Castle of Seemly Joy. A
woman's power had created it, and it was too much for my buddies. When I
looked back to see the expressions on their wheezy faces, they had disappeared. No great loss.

See, it was all so figurative around there that I wasn't letting anything
surprise me. I had my key ready, and lo and behold! it exactly fitted the
golden lock on the Castle's front door. I opened it and went in, feeling sort
of like Goldilocks, like you know? "Hellooo!" I called, but I guess nobody
was home. Nobody with lungs, anyway.

And there it was, the crystal Saint Nappie, just as I'd been told. It was
sitting on like this comfy-looking satin pillow. I reached out slowly, expecting like these horrible last-second Indiana Jones kind of traps to spring
loose all around me. My hand touched the berry bowl and I felt, like, glass,
huh? I picked up the bowl, and in that very instant the pillow, the table it

was resting on, the parlor, and the whole goddamn Castle of Seemly Joy disappeared. I was standing in the Pearly Path again. Even the nice meadow had gone with the wind.

It was just me and the Saint Nappie. I looked at it, you know, close up, and I saw these letters of fire along the rim. I peered even closer until I could read them. They said:

Hazel-Atlas Glass Company, Wheeling, West Virginia

Suddenly I had a terrible headache. I mean, like I had to wonder if all the derring-do had been worth it. Was this the very berry bowl used by Jesus at the Last Supper? Who could tell? The ways of the unreal and symbolic can be inexplicable, even to such a nimble and resourceful mind as mine.

I took a deep breath, let it out, and muttered, "Son of a—"

And then like uh-oh I whooshed right here to your car. And you know the most bizarre thing? I don't even have the Saint Nappie to show you! How's that for irony, huh?

YPICAL. Just too goddamn typical. I dropped Muffy off at Penn Station because she said she wanted to visit her mother, who had recently remarried. Before she left, she asked about Malachi Bret and how was I doing with a little rugrat to take care of. Muffy is not, you should know this, the maternal type. I told her I was doing just fine, that Josh was a great help with the baby, and that under no circumstances did I ever want my old Greenberg School chum to become Aunt Muffy. If I could work it, I'd make it so Malachi Bret never even heard the name Maureen Danielle Birnbaum.

Not that I really dislike Muffy. I guess I don't. I just think Malachi Bret ought to learn to handle a Louisville Slugger before he gets his hand on a full-tilt, blooded and ready-to-party broadsword.

Still, can you feature the expression on his first-grade teacher's face if he brought Old Betsy to school for show-and-tell? In Muffy's elegant words, "Wow, huh?"

Here's a brand-new (and perhaps final) Maureen Birnbaum story, written especially for this volume. I'd always wanted to pit my resourceful Mufferoo against the eldritch, ichorous evil of H. P. Lovecraft's Cthulhu mythos. I just hope I don't end up with tentacled abominations under my bed on account of it.

Maureen Birnbaum
at the Looming Awfulness

Maureen Birnbaum
at the Looming Awfulness

by Elizabeth Spiegelman

(as told to George Alec Effinger)

HAVE YOU EVER *had your life fall apart like a condominium of cards? I have, God knows. I know the feeling. One day I'm a happy wife and mother, married to my Josh, a successful doctor in Queens, New York. We doted on our baby son, Malachi Bret. Mums' aggravation I could keep to a minimum, and I couldn't have asked for more.*

We had just about everything a young, upwardly mobile family should have. We had two cars, both sleek, one cream and one fire-engine red. Our condo was in a predominantly non-ethnic neighborhood. We belonged to a very high-class health club, and we went there at least twice a month—we sat in the Jacuzzi, mostly. Josh did tennis now and then, and sometimes when I felt like it I did Richard Simmons. His video tapes, I mean. I had a glass-fronted cabinet stuffed with my favorite Mikasa china pattern in a complete service for sixteen. Josh's practice was growing so quickly that he had to take on a junior partner to handle the boring stuff.

Life was like good.

For a while.

One day Josh came home from his office and sat down heavily in a chair.

121

*There wasn't anything unusual in that because he always sat down heavily.
That's because he's—heavy. Quite a bit heavier than the slim and trim Josh I
married.*

*All right, I'm heavier, too. That's why we go to the health club every few
weeks. None of that is important, though. After Josh got comfortable enough,
he turned to me with an embarrassed smile. "Betsy," he goes, "there's something we've got to talk about."*

*Uh oh, I go. There are only a few times in your life when someone goes,
"There's something we've got to talk about." One time is when a cherished
friend or family member has slipped into an irreversible coma. This happens
on "Days of Our Lives" all the time. Somehow, though, I didn't think that
was the news that Josh was waiting to tell me.*

*"What is it, Josh?" I go, my voice all weak and like trembling. There'd
been a lot of changes—maybe too many—in my life lately. Like I'd been a
militant vegetarian for a while but I was cured by a bacon chili cheeseburger
with grilled onions from Bar's Mike and Grill not far from our house. And
my maroon Renault had gone to car hell because no one in town would work
on it, and Josh had bought me a cream '77 Fiat 124 Spider 'cause I'd always
wanted a little European roadster. It wasn't running so well, either.*

*So I was all set to hear that the condo association had raised its quarterly
fee, or that Josh was being sued by someone allergic to cotton swabs, or
some damn weird thing. What Josh told me, though, I wasn't prepared for at
all.*

*He gave me that puny smile again and goes, "Betsy, I'm desperately in
love with my receptionist, Candi Ann, and I can't live without her and I'm
leaving you for her and you and Malachi Bret have four weeks to find
someplace else to live."*

*That was the moment I knew Mums' assessment of Josh had been right all
along. He was scum or even lower than scum, whatever that might be.*

I smiled back at Josh and I go, "No, huh."

*I've learned a little bit about being a tough, 90s kind of gal from my
friend, Muffy. She, of course, was my long-ago-and-far-away best friend
from high school, Maureen Danielle Birnbaum. For sure, she absolutely
hates being called Muffy these days—though she thought it was like pretty
neat when those Andover and Exeter guys called her that. I tell her, I go, "If
you keep calling me Bitsy when I want to be called Elizabeth, you just got to
expect the same in return." I just laid it out for her.*

Actually, like the only important differences in our status is that my folks have more money *than hers, and Muffy has a* broadsword *and I don't, you know?*

So you got to let me explain about the broadsword. See, a while back, for some crazy reason I mostly fail *to believe, Muffy like transported herself spaceshipless to the Planet Mars, where she fought battles and won the undying love and respect of a* crushingly *handsome prince and his henchlings.*

Ever since, she's been trying to return to Mars and Prince Van, but although she manages to transport just fine, it's like she has no control over the destination. *It seems to make no difference, because she always ends up someplace exciting, and she has way rude adventures, and she always comes back here to regale and annoy me with her stories.*

Well, after Josh's lame announcement, I went over to stay with Mums and Daddy for a while. I sure couldn't stay in the condo with my faithless former ever-loving soulmate. And I took Malachi Bret with me. He was four years old now, and he just* loved *to color in the wall space around Mums' electrical outlets. I must admit that I thought he showed a certain de Chirico flair, but the effect was totally lost on Mums.*

Anyway, *I was lying on the bed in my old room. I was watching a "Geraldo" show about how blind people are struggling to deal with the designated driver concept. For some reason I thought this was the most* tragic *thing I'd ever heard of, and I couldn't stop crying. I had a box of Kleenex by one hand and a half-pound bag of malted milk balls by the other. Mums' cat, Loathing, was asleep on my feet. Her mate, Fear, was sitting on the TV, his fluffy tail hanging down in front of Geraldo's face. Mums swears that both of them hate the anthropocentrist word "cat," and prefer to be called "feline-Americans."*

I heard a sound. It was sort of a whuffle.

"It could be Santa," I thought. I was dubious, because it was only September. I turned toward the windows, and there was Muffy, still in her goddamn gold brassiere and G-string, still toting all the spoils from her various conquests, still dragging around Old Betsy, her broadsword. It's not named after me—I should be so honored—but because that's what Davy Crockett called his rifle.

"Yo, where you at, B?" she goes.

See, first she called me Bitsy, and then she called me Bits, which I hated in an ultimate *sort of way, and now it was just B. I wondered what would be next—just the Buh part, without the Ee.*

"Aw, Muffy," I go, "you practically promised you wouldn't come back here anymore."

She grinned her warrior-woman grin. "Fortunately, things changed miraculously, aren't you glad? And don't call me Muffy, okay?"

I took a deep breath and let it out in a sigh. "So where did you end up this time?"

She grinned again. "I'll give you a hint. To quote Groucho Marx in 'A Night at the Opera,'—boogie, boogie, boogie!"

You see what I mean? I cleverly hid the bag of malted milk balls under the covers. She wasn't going to get even one. For what it's worth, here's her stirring account.

THE MOST MERCIFUL THING in the world, I think, is the inability of my mind to remember things from one day to the next. I have had some startling and thrilling exploits—many more than you have recorded for the education of my audience—yet so often my adventure is made all the more arduous by what I have come to call "inappropriate forgetfulness."

In the mirror I still appear young, as young as I did when I studied at the Greenberg School; nevertheless, I sometimes wonder if I have developed an unusually premature case of Alzheimer's Disease. I get lost in jungles more easily than I care to admit, I sometimes forget the names of heroic people of both sexes, and likewise the villains, and I'm always leaving behind just those items that would substantiate the oral histories of my wonderful journeys, when I tell them to you, my dear friend, Blitzy Bitsy Spiegelman. Or Spiegelman-Fein. Or maybe it's just Spiegelman again these days. You've *got* to let me know which you want me to use.

I have just returned from an exploit filled with occult evil, wizardry, and terror beyond imagining. Alas, I—and one other—alone remain to tell the tale, and once more, alas, I have nothing to support my words but a bit of charred rope which I could have obtained anywhere.

Bitsy, have you *noticed* that my narrative style has become like, you know, dated, clumsy, and ornate? That I'm not talking in the airy colloquial phrases for which I'm justly celebrated? That is one of the insidious effects of my brush with . . . the *horror.* For now, that's the only way I can refer to it. I dare not name it until I have made the setting clear. Later you will know all, and you will wish that you did not. It will be my fault if your dreams are troubled for weeks and months to come, but I know how *eagerly* you look forward to these recitations of my courageous endeavors.

It all began in the Sterling Memorial Library at Yale University, like the largest open-stack library in the Free World. I saw your eyes open wider when I mentioned the college. I suppose as old as you get, you never lose the certainty that New Haven, Connecticut and Yale University are pretty much *Heaven* as far as we Greenberg School girls were concerned. Harvard was too stuffy, Princeton too rural, but *Yale*—and those gallant Yalies!—was what our education and training had prepared us for. We were to go forth and charm a Yalie into marriage; or else, if we failed, we tried to be satisfied entering matrimony with, oh, like a *family practitioner*, as you did.

Be that as it may, in my final (and I do mean like *final*) attempt to reach the boffable Prince Van on Mars, I stretched myself out toward Mars; instead, I hit that library in that university on the north shore of Long Island Sound. I realized that I was on Earth immediately, of course; I've had *other* exploits on Earth, but they've all been with mythical figures or in historical times. Now, however, I had dropped into the Sterling Memorial Library, and a newspaper there informed me that it was March 1, 1966.

I worried for a moment. I had *whooshed*, all right, but I hadn't whooshed very far in either time or space. This had been happening pretty often lately. The next time I whoosh, who knows but I may end up only an hour in the past, standing in my magnificent Amazonian regalia in Rabbi and Mrs. Gold's bedroom four houses down the block.

Did this mean that my career as the premier female swordsperson and all-around savior of men and women in distress had come to an *end?* Was I like *stuck* here, in the recent past in New Haven, forever? Well, it could have been worse. I could have journeyed back to Mars and discovered that Prince Van broke our dates all the time and never called the next day. He might have been interested in One Thing and One Thing Only, something I wouldn't like give up easily even to him. He might have wanted the two of us to go live with his *mother*, the queen, for God's sake.

I guess that as the years passed, and as my failures to return to Mars became embarrassingly numerous, my once-vivid memories of the glorious Prince Van began to fade. Also, I'd begun to suspect that the handsome prince didn't *want* to be found, and that I'd been put on some kind of interplanetary *Hold* or something.

Further, I might mention, I'd met another young man early in my adventures, a stalwart and courageous person of great intellect and daring. I was to meet him again during this shocking and unspeakable experience, although I did not know it when I first arrived, dressed in my fighting harness of skimpy leather and strands and strings of gold and jewels. I still wore my battle sword, Old Betsy, in her scabbard at my side, and my tangled hair and grim, warrior-woman expression left me pretty much out of place in the cool and quiet precincts of the Sterling Memorial Library.

In *fact*, security personnel were already hurrying toward me, either to like slaughter me where I stood or, at the very least, to eject me forcibly from the premises. As a fighting woman proud of her accomplishments and possessing superior combat skills, agility, and strength, I welcomed the challenge. It was only later that I realized that I'm *always* causing unnecessary uproar when I might fare better without making a scene at all.

This time, as usual, I *did* make a scene. Old Betsy sang as I whanged her from her scabbard. Immediately, all the security guards stopped in their tracks and pulled out their LFRs. LFRs are Little Radios; I don't need to tell you what the F word is, because it's *the* F word, and I just don't use language like that. People tell me that they're impressed that I can whoosh around the universe and have strange encounters all the time, and *still* remain like the sweet and innocent young lady I was years ago at the Greenberg School.

Discretion, as I've come to know, is somewhere between 56% and 64% of valor. I responded in my new and highly-regarded mature manner, and reassured the armed guards that I Meant Them No Harm. "There, there," I go, smiling and patting the air soothingly and behaving almost *completely* in a non-threatening way. Then I simply turned my back on the uniformed security personnel and made my way outdoors and into the late winter sunlight.

All right, I'd escaped from the world-renowned library, but my costume didn't work very well on the Old Campus, either. Especially in New Haven during this ancient era when even Carnaby Street was just too far-out for all of America northeast of Times Square. Remember that reaction you got from Miss Schildkraut, *Silas Marner* and Ninth Grade English, when you bought that *too-grotty-for-words* transparent plastic handbag? She was sure you were listening to drug-crazed moptop music and smoking banana peels *yourself*, too.

I had one immediate priority: a nice outfit from Ann Taylor Sportswear on Chapel Street, hard by the notorious Hotel Taft where many of our *consoeurs* have been overcome by passion and gin. I was thinking of a pale green, button-down collar shirtdress that I could wear through the spring, a pair of matching Jacques Cohen espadrilles, a Provencal print handbag from Pierre Deux, and like whatever accessories happened to catch my eye.

If the saleshuman who served me thought the ready-to-rumble costume I wore into the shop was even the *least* bit bizarre, she hid it well—particularly when I took out the largish stash of cash I kept hidden in its sanctum in the left cup of my gold bra. I'd sold some gold and jewels after the last time I saw you, and I was going to need the folding money. My stepmother Pammy's gold card, which was in my *right* cup, wouldn't do me any good in 1966. I don't know if they even had *BankAmericards* back then.

Good old Pammy, I thought, how long it had been since I'd *seen* her. Oh my *Gawd*, Bitsy, I just thought that she probably still hasn't finished paying off my shopping duel with that hard-bitten bitch, Maid Marian.

I could only hope that my family was proud of me.

Well, I was now clothed appropriately for New Haven—or I *thought* I was, until I stepped out into the in-like-a-lion March wind. It was pretty damn *cold*, Bitsy. Whatever my exploit was going to be, I was just about certain that I could use a good Republican cloth coat. Not that I'm necessarily a Republican—I am chiefly non-partisan in my politics, preferring to remain available to come to the aid of *anyone* in need regardless of race, ethnic origin, religion, or creed. It's just that here I was, back in 1966, and like Nixon wasn't even President yet, but he reminded me of that cloth coat comment and how he wouldn't give the goddamn *dog* back. History was really redundant the second time around.

I decided to book it over to the Yale Co-op, like totally *forgetting* that I was stuck temporarily in the dim, dark ages before Yale admitted female undergraduates, and the selection of women's merchandise was going to be minimal at best. Nevertheless, I got myself a mildly wildly colored ski jacket that I'd just *have* to be satisfied with and a sterling silver circle pin, which I'd forgotten to buy for my shirtdress at Ann Taylor's.

Then, *it* happened.

What *was* it, I hear you go in your shocked and like breathless voice. Yes, it was eerie and dreadful in the most *total* extreme, a nightmarish confrontation that made my blood run as cold as that time when I thought I'd gotten, *you know*, PG from French-kissing that crispo dude from Waite Hoyt Junior High. Sure, Bitsy, now you can look back on *that* and laugh, but what I witnessed in the Yale Co-op near the vinyl record section was too demented and ichorous and fiendish to ever pry a giggle from me.

It was that *guy*, that Rod Marquand.

Now don't go all ignorant on me. You remember him *very* well. He was the one who appeared suddenly while I was being held captive by that talking ape-monster, Yag-Nash. Rod had that submarine sort of thing that traveled through solid rock. His problem was that he was more interested in like fighting *crime* than in wrestling with *me*, and I guess I stormed out of his company in a well-rehearsed huff.

So, the question immediately presents itself for asking, what was Rod Marquand, boy-inventor extraordinaire, doing at the Yale Co-op *twenty full years* before our encounter at the center of the Earth, *and looking exactly the same as he had then?*

You see, now, there were only two possible answers. The first was that he drank the blood of innocent virgins to maintain his hideous and dreadful youth—but that was like scarcely possible, because he'd never made *move one* toward any of my arteries, and you know I'd given him plenty of opportunities.

The second answer was that he was immortal and ageless, as I myself seem to be. That was *another* reason that like screamed that Rod Marquand and I were perfect for each other, made for each other as few other couples have been through the whole sad parade of history.

Yet this Rod was like twenty years *younger* than the one I'd known during the Yag-Nash episode. He would be meeting me as if for the first time. That didn't tell me why he didn't recognize me at the Earth's core, twenty years later. I went to Dr. Bertram A. Waters of the Yale University Plasmonics Department for help in understanding what had happened. He gave me like this completely murky explanation. Here it is, as best as I can recall it:

"My dear Miss Birnbaum—" he goes.

I go—believe me—"I'm not your *dear* anything, pal."

He got this look on his face like someone had slipped the head of a banana slug into his bag of malted milk balls. See, Bitsy, I *know* you got them there under the covers. He goes, "I doubt if I'm your 'pal,' either, but I suppose it's just a figure of speech. In any event, Maureen—may I call you Maureen?"

"If you must," I go, wishing that he'd like just get on with it.

"How does one understand time? There are various ways of imagining it. And yes, time is mostly imaginary. Of course, events happen and they must have some matrix to happen in, if you follow me. One instant the electron is all excited, and the next instant it's emitted its photon and gone home." I swear, Bitsy, the guy leered at me. Take it from me, sweetie, Mo *knows* leering for sure.

And don't *ever* call me "Mo."

Dr. Waters told me that he thought of time—everyone's personal time-line—as a string that stretches from Point A to Point Z. Now, if sometime somebody figures out how to travel *back* in time, the string goes from Point A to, say, Point L, loops back to Point G, maybe, then turns back through Point L—*in a different place*—and on again to Point Z. So if you meet a guy at Point G who is or will be a time-traveler, there's no telling if this is like his first or second pass through that moment. And there can be any number of trips into the past by the same chrononaut, looping again and again at Point G or any other point. Trust me on this, Bitsy, 'cause I took the trouble to consult experts.

No? Well, never mind, because I mean Dr. Waters wasn't completely sold on his own theory, and neither was I.

BTW—that's "by the way," by the way—I described what I'd seen in the Yale Co-op a bunch of ways, including ichorous. I may have exaggerated *un petit peu*, but Rod Marquand is on the far side of ichorous, and I should know.

Suddenly, when I saw him standing there, I wondered how I was going to meet him. I understood without even really thinking about it that it wasn't just a coincidence—Rod was here and we were going to have an exploit together, like before at the center of the Earth, only this time would technically be the first.

So I grabbed the nearest object—it happened to be the Beatles' newly-released album *Rubber Soul*—and I walked right up to him. My God, Bitsy, you *know* I've never been shy around boys. I think it's one of the things they admire most about me. That and my broadsword.

Well, I go, "Have you heard this album yet?"

Rod blinked at me—oh, he was T.C.T.L.! Too cute to live, honey, just try to stay with me—and he goes, "It's their best so far, I think. It's fab and groovy."

I smiled a little at his antique slang; on him it was like *real, real* sweet. I go, "I've heard some of it on the radio. What do you think 'Norwegian wood' really means?"

"It could be a code, you know," Rod goes. "An encryption of some enigmatic message known only to the Beatles themselves and their inner-most circle."

I sighed. "I wish *I* could be in that circle. I wish *I* could be Jane Asher." I remembered that in 1966 I had a crush on Paul, the cute one.

"Well," goes Rod, "their music is really neat, but at the moment there are more important things competing for my time and attention." As buf and tuf as Rod Marquand is, he's more of a party *vegetable,* if you get my drift. Sometimes I think he'd have to ask a girl to give him lessons before he could even be a *wallflower.*

"I'd like to know what those things are," I go, smiling my never-miss dreamy smile, Number Five at 75% power.

"If I'm not being too forward," Rod goes, completely conquered, "I'd like to invite you to have dinner with me at my residential college."

"What college are you in?"

"Branford," he goes, with an unspoken "of course" appended at the end.

It wasn't like a very *long* walk from the Co-op to the High Street entrance to Branford College, but I *mean!* The wind had picked up and now rain mixed with sleet had begun falling. I was damn glad I'd had the foresightfulness to buy the ski jacket. Rod put his hand under my elbow, evidently believing he was doing the yo-ho *manly* thing and helping me walk on the slippery pavement.

I simply shrugged away and smiled prettily and I go, "I'm so sure I can walk just fine by myself, thanks. Like I've only been *doing* this since I was a baby and everything."

He got a wounded puppy look on his face and maybe it was good for him. I told myself that I couldn't really expect a 90s kind of guy in 1966, but then I decided that it was never too soon to put somebody in touch with his real self.

We passed through the ironwork gate of Branford College, beneath the vasty, shadowed heights of Harkness Tower and The World's Most Illegible Clock. It was dinner time and I was *ravenous.* I hadn't eaten since twenty-seven years in the future.

"It looks like salisbury steak and two veg," Rod goes.

"Oh, we have that all the time at the Greenberg School," I go.

He smiled down at me and goes, "Not the way they make it here. We've got Jonathan Edwards' own recipe."

"Jonathan Edwards?" I thought he might have been a disk jockey on WABC-AM in the mid-60s.

"'Sinners in the Hands of an Angry God.' *That* Jonathan Edwards. There's another residential college named after him across the way."

Like *nothing* makes salisbury steak, two veg, and chocolate milk go down better than contemplating "Sinners in the Hands of an Angry God." I remembered something about spiders dangling on thin strands of web above the hellfire.

130

The evening proceeded to get ever more weird and romantic from that point on.

We'd finished eating and Rod put one hand on mine. He gazed into my eyes and goes, "Want some dessert?"

"I've told you that I'm a warrior-woman," I go. We'd gone through all that during the walk from the Co-op. I'd unwrapped Old Betsy and given him a hot look at my auric underwear. "I have to guard constantly against putting on weight, but I suppose a serving of bread pudding and some more chocolate milk wouldn't hurt me *too* much."

"Bread pudding?" Rod goes. "Why, that's my favorite dessert!" We just had *so much* in common.

That led to a discussion of the codification of all types of bread pudding, according to the official Ivy League definition. The chart looked something like this:

	YES	NO
Hot		
Cold		
Whiskey Sauce		
Rum Sauce		
Firm		
Fluffy		
With Raisins		
Without Raisins		

In 1966, the sixteen possible combinations like totally described bread pudding as science understood it at that point in time. Today, of course, with high-speed computers and the other miracles given to us by the space program, there are bread pudding types that were unimaginable during the Lyndon Johnson administration. For example, the best bread pudding I've ever had is served in the Palace Cafe on Canal Street in New Orleans, and it comes with a fantastic white chocolate sauce. In the 60s, such a thing would've been as illegal as beans in chili.

We found ourselves holding hands as we went back through the Branford cafeteria line. We each got a serving of bread pudding (hot, rum, fluffy, with raisins, and extremely good). When we returned to our table, Rod goes, "Hello! What's this?"

It was a page of photocopy paper, the strange, stark copies they turned out in the early days of the industry.

I tried to read the writing on the page, but it was in some strange, occult language. There were nightmarish drawings of nameless, hideous, tentacled creatures. I shuddered and gave the paper back to Rod.

He stared at the writing for a few moments, and then began to murmur, "Dead is not that which can through ages lie, to see in fell times how even death may die."

Gave me the shivering *creeps*, know what I mean, Bitsy? Not so my Hot Rod. He just shook his head. "Somebody's been playing some twisted joke on me lately, Maureen," he goes. "This isn't the first time I've gotten a copy of what the prankster wants me to think is some demented, malevolent manuscript."

"You can read it, though?" I go. I pretended to show interest in Rod's hobbies, because Miss Kanon, the gym teacher, always told us that would make us popular with boys. It always worked for me.

"Yes," Rod goes, "it's an old dialect of Arabic. I studied it one summer when my uncle, Dr. Zach Marquand, took me to Egypt to help solve the Mystery of the Dismembered Murderers."

"And you think someone is sending you joke messages in an obscure, ancient dialect? *Why?*"

Rod's adorable face suddenly went like all *serious*, you know? "I can't say for sure. The first was just a scrap, with the words *Cthulhu fhtagn* written on it. This 'Cthulhu' has been mentioned again and again. I don't know what it means."

I shuddered, even in the bright warmth of the Branford dining hall. "Cthulhu fhtagn," I go, all thoughtful. "It sounds *Gaelic* to me, not Arabic."

"It's neither," Rod goes.

"Maybe," I go, shivering again, "maybe it's the long-dead language of those scaly, unclean squid-headed creatures."

Rod didn't even respond to that notion. "Then there were all the references to the Sunken City of R'lyeh, and some blasphemous, horrible fertility goddess called Shub-Niggurath. And pages and pages of drawings and scraps of incomprehensible poetry and . . . *warnings.*"

I'll confess, Bitsy, my stomach started to hurt. "Listen, Rod," I go, "why don't we forget about Cthulhu tonight and just go see Michael Caine in *Alfie.* It's showing at the College for a buck and a half."

"Yes," he goes, folding the photocopy paper and tucking it into an inside pocket of his sport coat. "I'm not going to let some minor-league mentality get the better of me. I'm just going to ignore the entire business."

"Fine," I go. "Let's boogie."

"Let's . . . what?"

I stood up and he got up, too. "I'll let you carry my broadsword. I never let just *anybody* do that, you know."

We had a nice time at the movie, although Michael Caine's character was like this *pig*. Afterward, we went someplace for a light supper, and Rod installed me in the Hotel Taft. I shuddered alone in my bed, imagining that I could hear the helpless shrieks of my overpowered sisters as they were assaulted by tentacled fiends from R'lyeh wearing blue J. Press blazers and gray slacks.

I had fallen fast asleep, and *believe* me, Bitsy, my dreams were populated by obscene monsters that spoke in a Cockney accent. When my phone rang, I sat upright, terrified. I didn't know where I was or what time it was or *anything*. I answered the phone, sure that I was going to hear nothing but whistling, blubbery monster noises.

Instead, Rod goes, "Maureen? I hope I didn't wake you up."

It was one-thirty in the morning. "No, don't worry about it. I was just like sleeping."

"Good. Now, listen closely. When I returned to my rooms, I discovered several strange and ominous signs. First, my roommate, Sandy, was nowhere to be found. You have to understand that Sandy is terribly incompetent socially, and he usually retires to his bedroom shortly after dinner. It's entirely unlike him to be out so late."

I wasn't as upset about it as Rod was, but after all, I didn't know Sandy. "Maybe he's fallen in love with a forgiving townie woman," I go. "Or maybe he just really needed a burger or something."

Rod ignored my simple explanations. "Further," he goes, "the casement windows were forced open *from the inside*. Upon closer inspection, I found traces of a horrible, foul-smelling slime on the window sill, and it was dripping and oozing down the outside wall to the ground."

"Slime," I go in a flat voice. I just *knew* we were going to run into slime somewhere along the way. Greenberg School girls are, as you know, Bitsy, antipathetic toward slime in general.

"The last dreadful clue was that the trail of slime led right to Harkness Tower. The door had been burst open, and as I entered and looked up the stairwell that led to the clock tower and carillon, I noted a diffuse and flickering greenish light descending from the highest level."

"Calm down, Rod," I go. "Now tell me why you called *me* about all this."

"Well, Maureen," he goes—and I could tell that he was like *way* embarrassed—"I am inclined to take those notes, drawings, and warnings more seriously. My theory is that one of those eldritch evils abducted Sandy with foul intent, and has dragged him to the top of Harkness Tower. I called you because—"

"—because *I'm* the one with the broadsword," I go. "Okay, I'll get dressed and be right there."

Immediately I had like this gross image problem: The proper costume to accompany Old Betsy was the metallic bra and G-string, of course. We're talking New England winter, though, and if I got into my familiar barbarian drag, I'd freeze my *tush* off. And the alternative—wearing the Ann Taylor shirtdress with the broadsword—was too ludicrous even to *consider*.

I compromised. I wore the leather harness and gold bikini, and zipped up the ski jacket over them. I hefted Old Betsy, made sure I had my hotel key and bus fare, and headed out fearlessly into the night.

By the time I got to Branford and the entrance to the chapel in the base of Harkness Tower, my legs had goosebumps the size of loquats, I'm telling you. My Rod was waiting for me. He rushed to me and enclosed me in his arms. "Don't be afraid, my dear," he goes. "I've picked up some spells along the way that I'm confident will protect us against most of the perverse beings we may meet up there."

"*Most?*" I go. I shuddered. I really wished he hadn't said 'most.'

"If you guard my back," he goes, "I'll lead the way." He was so brave! Finally, here was a man I could *respect*.

I also wasn't crazy about his use of the word 'spells.' He was introducing at this late date a severely *fantastic* element into what had been—except for that Saint Graal business, which was no doubt just the nightmare effect of a late-night pizza or something—*clearly* a super-scientific series of adventures. I explained my objection to Rod.

"I'm dead certain that there's a super-scientific explanation to *this,* too," he goes. "We just have to find out what it is. Come on, now."

I wasn't crazy about his use of the term '*dead* certain,' while we're at it.

"I've got a flashlight, Maureen," Rod goes bravely. "A lot of predatory animals *flee* bright light."

"Oh yeah," I go. "How many slime-trailing, sleepless, slimy, slobbering things do you know that will *run and hide* from your Eveready?"

"Okay," he goes, "you've put your finger on the major difficulty of our expedition here. We're up against the unknown, and we can't predict how successful our conventional fighting techniques will be. It may be that my spells and your broadsword ability will avail us naught against the poisonous entities from beyond the stars. But I ask you, what *else* can we do?"

I didn't hesitate long, let me tell you. "We could wait for help in the morning. We could consult more learned authorities on campus—and *surely* there are a few paraphysicists who could help us. We could give your roommate up for lost and go have *breakfast* in a short while. We could hope that Cthulhu or whoever is intruding on our peace might just decide to look around and go home. There are *any* number of other courses of action beside *going up this spiral stairwell.*"

"Let's climb, anyway," Rod goes. "There isn't much other choice."

"As long as *you'll* take the first attack from beyond the stars. That will give me time to scramble back down the stairs. Just *kidding*, of course."

We did climb nearer and nearer the carillon bells, and nothing more disturbing interrupted us for a time. After a while, however, the carillon began to sway a bit in the non-existent breeze, clapping together and making strange, unearthly, *ancient-sounding* bell melodies. At the same time, I noticed that pulsating, poisonous patterns were written out on the stone walls in nacreous, glowing runes that neither Rod nor I could identify, as well as terrible, twisting pictographs that moved of their own accord. They writhed before us, and we had no way of knowing how to interpret them.

There were overwhelmingly strong hints of monsters, of gods or creatures from beyond our time and space. I wondered how we could *possibly* understand them—and if we couldn't understand them, then how could we battle them? Were we *doomed* to become slaves to their will?

No. I'll let you know that right *up front*, Bitsy. At this point in the investigation, the manifold forms of the The Great Old Ones did *not* possess us. We had a means of escape. Let me tell you about it.

Rod had apparently studied many of the subtexts that dealt with the rites of the Great Old Ones, as well as others that involved the Outer Gods and other alien races and monsters.

There *were*, unfortunately, many, many classes of ancient, unknown, inhuman, mind-numbing gods. The one encountered by me and good old Rod was called a Dark Young of Shub-Niggurath. Though less formidable than some of the other Outer Gods, it still appeared in a *horrible, unspeakable, repellent* form.

It was a gigantic, grasping thing, a hideous animated "tree" with poisonous tentacles for branches; the tentacles ended in black hooves, and the creature could shamble clumsily across the ground. It had many puckered mouths, each dripping the same gruesome green slime we'd seen in Rod's Branford suite. The Dark Young reeked like an opened grave, and it towered over us some fifteen feet tall. I'll tell you once, dear, it was certainly not *pleasant* in any respect.

Rod was prepared, however; he knew a brief cantrip that freed us from the horror of the Dark Young. I didn't understand a *word* of the spell, as it was spoken in some lost language that delighted in words ending in— vowel-t-h and other vocabulary that was so guttural that you could get gall stones just *listening* to it. My Greenberg School dabbling into European dialects was hardly enough to keep me informed of what was happening.

Anyway, the Dark Young seemed to freeze. It became absolutely motionless, and then began to shrink. To me, it looked like it was disappearing down a dark, featureless tunnel. We didn't wait around long enough to see what would happen next. "Follow me, sweetheart," I cried, and I led the way down the staircase and out of the tower. You must know by now that I have no problem being decisive and, anyway, I didn't want that green goo all over my trusty broadsword.

I realized that I'd been holding my breath, and it was good to inhale deeply in the fresh, cold air of the Branford courtyard. "I'll see you back to the Taft," Rod goes. "First thing in the morning, we'll pay a call on the Sterling Library. I believe they have some texts that will help understand what's happening here."

I nodded. Of course, I yearned to get into battle, but I was also wise enough to realize that we had some homework to take care of first. "What about Sandy, your roommate?" I go.

Rod rubbed his strong, square chin. "I think Sandy is the prisoner of some greater, more grotesque evil. The Dark Young was there merely to stall us, or to frighten us into giving up the chase."

"Fear?" I go, laughing. "It's not even in my primary word-list. I'll meet you here at nine-thirty tomorrow morning. I want to get myself a pair of jeans, a sweatshirt, and some good sneakers. I don't want to go up against the Vast Unclean from Dimension X in an Ann Taylor shirtdress."

"Whatever you say, Maureen," he goes. "The forces of the profane will be patient."

That made me shudder despite myself.

Time passes. That's a *quote*, by the way, Bitsy, and a Snickers bar if you can tell me where it comes from. Give up? Dylan Thomas, *you* remember. Time passes. It's morning, I bopped by the Co-op again and got myself some horrible new stiff blue jeans, a blue sweatshirt with "Yale University" printed in teeny tiny letters—reverse ostentation, I called it—and some canvas gym shoes. This was in the Nouveau Stone Age before Reeboks, you know. I'm wearing the ski jacket and carrying the shirtdress in a bag with Old Betsy. I was ready to *get down*. As it were.

Well, I trudged back to High Street and Branford College. I have to admit that I suppressed another shudder as I passed beneath Harkness Tower, but it was daytime now and bright and warm under the sun, and the Dark Young of Shub-Niggurath might have been just some black-and-white monster from a movie somewhere between Godzilla and Mothra.

Hey, did you ever wonder how, when a new monster appears in Japan, the people immediately know its *name?* I figured it out. They have a list, like with hurricanes. A new monster gets the next name on the list. The giant turtle appears and everybody goes, *"Ohhh,* Gammera the Invincible!" It's simple if you understand the Asian point of view. Well, of *course* I do, what do you know about it?

Rod was waiting for me in the courtyard, fidgeting a little. "Good morning, Maureen," he goes. He like gave me a chaste, heroic kiss on the cheek. Jeez, he was almost perfect!

"Let's do it," I go. My voice was deep and rumbly. I was fully in my fighting-woman persona again.

We walked to the Sterling Memorial Library. This time when I went in, no one made a fuss. I looked like Suzy Co-Ed, even though, as I've mentioned, Yale hadn't yet got its act together about that. Maybe the librarians and security guards all believed I was some Smith or Bennington talent down for a few days.

Rod murmured to me, "The texts we need to consult are in a special section, the Omega Collection. They're generally not available to the public, but I'm a good friend of the curator. I've used that material before, and I'll explain to Dr. Christenson that this is an emergency. He'll understand."

About a quarter of an hour later, a very old, very fragile book came down a dumbwaiter for us. It was so ancient, it could've been like the first rough draft of the Old Testament, you know? Rod treated it with caution and great respect, and carried it over to a table where we could browse through its mystic text.

"This is an English translation of the *Necronomicon,*" Rod goes, "hand-copied from Dr. John Dee's original manuscript sometime in the last two or three centuries. It is extremely rare, and literally priceless in value. It's a very great honor to be allowed to view this book."

"Well," I go, *"I'm* suitably impressed."

137

"This is also the source of the photocopied drawings and inscriptions that I've received," he goes. He turned a few pages. "Hello! What's this?"

Another photocopy had been inserted between two of the book's crumbling pages. It said, "R.M."—that must have stood for "Rod Marquand," I guessed—and then some numbers. "What does it mean?" I go.

"If I'm correct, this is a certain longitude and latitude. We'll need to consult an accurate atlas next."

"Is it a warning?" I go. "Or a *challenge?*"

Rod gazed at me steadily. "Perhaps both," he goes. He didn't show the least hint of fear.

A few minutes later, we'd established the location indicated on the photocopy. The city of New Haven, Connecticut is hemmed in by two large ridges, West Rock and East Rock. Both are easily climbed, with roads twisting back and forth from their bases to their summits. They make for pleasant hiking in the spring and fall.

The intersection of longitude and latitude fell right at the topmost point of East Rock. "There," Rod goes, stabbing his finger down on the map, "*that's* where we'll find *It*. And, I hope, my roommate Sandy."

Rod had a bicycle and he borrowed another for me, and together we pedaled toward our grim destination. I was completely lost, because I didn't know New Haven very well beyond the immediate environs of the university. It was too early in the season for the journey to be picturesque. No flowers bloomed, and the oaks and elms loomed above us naked and black in their leaflessness.

It was good warrior-woman exercise, though, and I could feel the burn in my mighty thews as I pushed the Italian ten-speed up the long slope of East Rock. I've found that just as everyone in the universe *miraculously* speaks English, and that I *miraculously* never seem to age, also *miraculously* I rarely put on too much weight. Oh, there'll be a pound or two now and then around the holidays or after some wanton barbarian feast, but my active life has toned me up much better than your exclusive health club seems to have done for you. No offense, Bitsy, of *course* I'm not being catty.

"Look, there!" Rod goes. He was like freaking out on me.

I stared where he was pointing, and I couldn't see a goddamn *thing*. He dragged his bike across the road, and I followed. When I got closer, I saw why he was so excited. He'd discovered a small crack in the rock that proved to be the entrance to a noxious, noisome, unspeakable cavern.

Lord only knows how many thousands of people had passed right by that place, but it took the eagle eye of Rod Marquand to spot the significant opening. I knew there was nothing in the Yale student guide to New Haven about noxious, noisome, unspeakable caves. Unspeakable rival schools, maybe, but nothing about caves.

"We're getting close," he goes. "I can feel it."

It was dark, and there were webby things hanging down in my face. "It sure is unspeakable in here," I go. "Indescribable, too."

"Don't talk, Maureen," he goes. "Save your energy for *It.*"

"What is this *It* we're going to be going up against?" I go. "Can you give me an idea?"

Rod's voice came from further into the cavern, whose floor had begun to slope upward. "Perhaps Great Cthulhu himself. There's no way of knowing. I hope you have a tight grasp on your sanity."

"I've got a tight grasp on Old Betsy," I go. "She's always been enough for me so far."

"You've never been confronted by one of the Slobbering Obscene before."

"Except last night," I go, reminding him. He did not answer. That bothered me, too.

I could not see Rod, so I trudged along behind him. It had become stiflingly warm inside the cave, and I unzipped the ski jacket. I wanted to drop the jacket altogether, because I could better wield my sword without it, but I thought, *"Hey.* What if we run into the Ice Abomination from the Moons of Pluto?" *Better safe than sorry* is the motto of our wing of the Birnbaum clan, you know.

Ahead of me I heard Rod go "Courane? Is that you?" There was an awful moment of silence, and then he goes, "My God, Sandy! What's *happened* to you?"

I go, *"Oh boy,* here we go. Get yourself ready for Interstellar Pudding Monsters."

In a marvelous testimony to my innate courage and like sheer, overwhelming *gutsiness,* I did not hesitate. I hurried along until I beheld the excruciating, festering creature that Rod's friend had become.

"It must have been the contact with the Great Old Ones," Rod goes in a frantic, fearful voice.

Sandy had become a gnarled, aged man, lurching and clutching blindly in the flickering greenish glow emanating from some sort of well in the midst of the cavern. His hair had turned white and most of it had kind of fallen out, you know? And he drooled a weird substance that was truly, truly *ichorous.* He could barely be called human anymore, and if it were up to me, I *wouldn't* have. Yet, after all, he was still in some way connected to his elder self—Rod's companion and roommate.

"I can't stand it!" Rod goes. "Maureen, beware! That which caused this change in Courane lies nearby, and you risk the soundness of your mind should you chance to make contact with it!" I thought Rod's speech had taken a sharp turn into the *melodramatic,* but I didn't say anything about that.

Around Sandy floated odd shapes—illusions, lesser monsters, or thought-projected weapons I could not tell. They looked like . . . well, apart from being indescribable, they looked like drab-colored, hovering paisleys.

"*Paisleys,* Rod!" I go. "Sandy is trying to tell us something!"

"Tell us something? *How?* And what is he trying to say?"

"I don't *know!*" I go. Like I was putting most of my attention on what had once been your average college student. I didn't want to hurt Sandy, but I knew that I might have to, in order to like save our lives. I concentrated my attack on the paisleys. There were red paisleys, blue ones, and green ones. That cavern looked like an explosion in the Land's End tie factory.

I learned very quickly that when I whacked a floating paisley, it became *two* small floating paisleys. Something told me that it would be like ever so harmful to let one of them touch us. I backed away a little more. The Sandy-creature took a step forward, and the paisleys advanced with him.

"Be careful!" Rod goes helpfully. "He's trying to cut us off from the way out!"

I'd already noticed that, but then, of course, I'm a fierce fighting-person, well-schooled in hand-to-hand combat, and therefore much better informed than Rod in such warlike mysteries as strategy and tactics. Instead of slashing at the nearest paisley, I just poked it a little. Just to see what happened.

It exploded. Into about a thousand micro-paisleys. "Jeez," I go. I was starting to be troubled.

"He's *humming!*" Rod goes, all excited. "He's humming some spell!"

"What is it? What's it mean? You got a counter-spell?"

I couldn't see Rod, but his voice was sad. "No," he goes. "Unfortunately, it's in the one Aramaic dialect I neglected in my studies. Wouldn't you just know it?"

"Great," I muttered through my clenched teeth.

Onward Sandy came. Further back the floating paisleys pressed us. I could feel the low wall of the gruesome well against my legs. Rod and I retreated further. *"Help me, Rod!"* I go.

At about this very moment, Rod decided he'd had enough, and he de-invited himself from the remainder of this confrontation. I did not hold it against the dear young man. This may have been his first meeting with such an onslaught of demonic activity, and he did not have either the experience or the fierce determination that I had.

Further into the gloom we stumbled. I felt a single moment of despair, and then *suddenly* I knew just what to do, as usual. I understood that I had to capture Courane's attention, and I had to appeal to the small crumb of human intelligence that still remained to him, unsullied by the dire alien influences.

"Sandy," I go, *"paisley!* Think paisley! I know what you're trying to tell us. If you concentrate, I know I can pull you out of this horrible mind-control."

"Yeah?" goes Rod.

I ignored him for the moment. "Sandy, think about your paisley ties! Think Ivy League, think crocodiles, think Lacoste shirts! Think Branford! Above all, think *Yale!"*

Courane roared and staggered back. He brought his twisted, knotted hands to his face, and he fell to one knee.

"I think you're on the right track, Maureen," goes Rod.

"You bet." I swung Old Betsy low, and she whanged off the fetid stone of the glowing green well. Sandy's eyes opened a little wider, and he crawled back another short distance.

"Remember the Clock at the Biltmore!" It still existed in this time, I knew. "Think *L. L. Bean,* Sandy! And will Great Cthulhu supply you with gin and tonics? I think *not!"* He was on both knees now, clawing at me either in supplication or in a fevered, fiendish attempt to rip open my throat. I wish you'd seen me, Bitsy. I was like *stupendous.*

"You think you'll get into a super-secret senior society like Skull and Bones like this, Sandy?" I go. Well, maybe he could.

Finally, unable to withstand the fury of my psychological attack any longer, he scrambled to his feet, uttered a long, ululating, despairing cry, and hurled himself over the brink of the demonically gleaming well. I heard his shriek echo from the walls for what seemed many minutes. With his last ounce of humanity, Sandy had sacrificed himself for us.

Then there was like this *silence,* okay?

The floating paisleys had disappeared. The sense of foreboding gave way to, well, boding. The permeating atmosphere of absolute evil lifted. Rod got to his feet, shaking his head. "What . . . what happened?" he goes.

I took him by the hand. "Come along, dear," I go. "We have a long bike ride home."

And that, pretty simply, is how I overcame the worst that the ancient, amorphous, deathless, eldritch, gibbering gods of Elsewhere and Elsewhen threw at me. I guess I'm just too solidly centered in Real Life to be driven crazy by a bulbous and mouldering octopoid. I figured I chased them all back to Massachusetts, where they belonged.

SO," SHE GOES, "what do you think?"

"What do I think?" I go. "I think my life is over. I think my husband has left me for his receptionist, I think my baby son doesn't have a father anymore, I think I may have to move in with Mums and Daddy practically forever, and I think I don't give a good goddamn what you do with your sword."

Muffy just stared at me for a moment. "Do you mean it?" she goes.

"Yeah, I mean it."

"I mean, like you've been testy before, God knows, but I could always count on you, Bitsy."

"Elizabeth, please. Call me Elizabeth."

Muffy looked like a shelf of books had dumped on her head. "You'll get over it," she goes. "Sure, you will."

I dabbed at my nose with a tissue. "Go haunt somebody else for a while," I go.

She smiled sadly and shook her head. "I'm going to go find Rod Marquand, and we're going to continue our everlasting romance, and we're going to get married and be happy forever, and I'm going to want you to be my matron of honor, so you've got to get over this depression, Bitsy. C'mon, just cheer up!"

I almost threw a shoe at her, except I didn't have a shoe. She blew me a kiss, walked out of my bedroom, and I haven't seen or heard from her since.

Thank you, Lord.

A Little Lagniappe

"Lagniappe" is an old French word still in use in southern Louisiana. It means "a little something extra." Like in the good old days, when a baker would toss in a free thirteenth doughnut when you bought a dozen.

I wrote "Maureen Birnbaum's Lunar Adventure" a number of years ago, just for a science fiction convention's program book. I forgot about it entirely until I began putting this collection together, and I thought I'd toss it in just for fun.

The story's for Reginald Bretnor, who perfected the form.

Maureen Birnbaum's
Lunar Adventure

Maureen Birnbaum's Lunar Adventure

by Elizabeth Spiegelman

(as told to George Alec Effinger)

ERE'S HOW MUFFY BIRNBAUM ruined my life again. *About three years had passed since her ichorous meeting with the Mollusk-Arthropod Yuck Monsters from Beyond Space and Time. I had already begun to slip in to an always-dangerous sense of security, believing that Maureen had kept her word, gone off Planet X with the love of her life, and was busily raising young Muffins like a normal person.*

In her words, N. S. L. No such luck. I'd just looked at my watch, so I knew it was almost precisely noon. I was sitting in a pink molded-plastic chair, waiting for my job interview at some manufacturing firm. I was applying for the position of Pocket Fisherman assembler. It was a high-tech, high-skill job that commanded your basic minimum wage.

About 12:03 I saw Maureen Danielle Birnbaum de-whoosh noisily into the blue plastic chair beside me. "Sorry I'm late," she goes. She was out of breath.

I didn't say anything. I pretended I didn't know her. She was wearing her gold brassiere and G-string, carrying Old Betsy, her broadsword, in one hand and a NASA spacesuit over the other.

"Wait 'til I tell you—" she goes.

"Please, Maureen, don't talk to me. They'll think I know you. I'm desperate for this job."

"If it's money, honey," she goes, "I can pry loose another emerald for you. No big deal."

I glared at her, remembering what had happened with the last emerald. Then I stood up and walked to the receptionist's desk. "Will it be much longer?" I go.

She goes, "Let me see." She talked to someone on the phone, hung it up, and muttered, "It'll be just a few more minutes."

I just nodded. I went back and sat down beside Muffy, but I didn't give her so much as a sideways glance. I couldn't help hearing her moving account of her personal conquest of the moon, though. You'd think she would've been just a little embarrassed.

Not Muffy. Never Muffy.

SO AFTER THE battle was over and my psychological wounds healed, I decided to whoosh out of the recent past and maybe try to find Mars again. I know I said I was going to forget about Prince Van, but I felt I owed him at least a tearful goodbye. It was just that he had been so overawed by me sexually that I had just a teensy amount of guilt about ruining him for the rest of his life as far as other women were concerned.

Anyway, from the Earth's 1966 I aimed at Mars, but I landed instead inside this big old domed research station on the moon. Now, *you* know and *I* know we don't have a research station on the moon. And like at first I thought it was, you know, a secret *Russian* thing or something. There was one large building inside broken up into separate laboratories, and like another building that was the dormitory and cafeteria and all. I wandered around, wondering where everybody was. I went through what looked like a chemistry lab, and then a geology lab, and all these other boring superscience setups. After a while I figured out that everybody must be asleep. It was the middle of the "night" there. So I left the lab building and checked out the other one. There was a coffee pot set up in the cafeteria, so I sat at a long table and drank a cup and thought. Like I can't remember the last time I was in such a fully beige place. *B-O-R-I-N-G,* all right? In an hour or so this guy comes into the cafeteria, gets himself a cup of coffee, looks at me and nods, and goes out. Like, who did he think I *was?* He didn't even wonder how I got *into* this big dome on the moon. You know, do they get a lot of visitors just dropping by there or what? That had me like totally freaked.

This place was *so* bogue, like they had a soda machine that sold only two things: Diet Water and New Coke, can you *believe* it? Like being on the moon wasn't *bad* enough. And there were Trivial Pursuit games sitting in their boxes on every table, as if they hadn't already *memorized* every one of the damn answers.

On a bulletin board was a mimeographed—*mimeographed*, Bitsy!— newsletter dated August 21, 2019, so I was truly back in the future, but not in the far future, like after the nuclear free-for-all I now knew was coming . . . sometime. This green dome belonged to the "Project Hephaestus, Joint NASA-Private Sector Lunar Industrial Feasibility Experiment 3, Col. Robert L. Jennings, Project Director." It was nice to know that when I found my way back to 1993, I could look forward to at least another twenty-six years until the Edgartown Regatta would be canceled due to inclement glowing mushroom clouds.

More people began coming in and getting coffee. It was fun to watch. This was the moon, right? The gravity was teeny compared with even the low gravity there was on Mars. The coffeepot was specially designed with a bigger pourspout, but you still had to wait until the coffee *felt* like doing its thing. You held the cup real close and tried to like *glug* it out. It moved slower and splashed higher. It took a while to get the hang of it. I didn't bother.

When it was officially morning or something, the kitchen help showed up and started cooking. Like this L.I.F.E. mission had brought their own little old cafeteria ladies. They must have hired them right out of some high school, because they had a little board set up with white plastic letters for the menu and everything. Before they changed it, it said Dinner: *Salisbury Steak, Choice of Veg $6.26.* Cafeteria food will *not* be a Miracle of the Future, honey, but inflation will be there to make us feel right at home. I did not have salisbury steak among the Horseclans, for which I suppose I must thank the nuclear war; no titanic cataclysm is *so* bad that it doesn't have its good points. I got in line and got ham and toast and eggs and grits. I tried to separate the stuff to find out what an individual *grit* was, but like I couldn't do it. I didn't want to eat it, anyway.

After brekky, this Colonel Jennings gets up and makes a speech. He tells us how *wonderful* we all were, and we applauded. He told us news from Earth, about how the New Orleans Indians had beaten the New Jersey

Yankees in a doubleheader and were now in first place. Apparently that was the most important thing on everyone's mind. I don't know, sweetie, I feel about baseball the same way I do about grits. Unless you're a major American literary figure or Huey Lewis and the News, baseball is like, you know, for *geeks*. But then I remembered I was in the future, and when you're in the future you have to live according to their ways. Who knows, maybe back home they had substituted the sports pages for the bicameral legislative system or something. We might wake up one morning and find the government divided into the Executive Branch, the Judicial Branch, and the NCAA.

So this Jennings dude starts to give all the labcoats in the audience their instructions for the day. It felt like *homeroom*, you know what I mean? Turns out that the scientists were mostly of the rocks and stars variety. For obvious reasons, I guess the what-you-call life sciences were like thinly represented. Actually, there was only this doctor and a pharmacist's mate along to take care of accidents and emergencies.

At the end the colonel goes, "The topographic survey people have requested additional manpower to help open up Area 76B and adjacent Area 78A. There seems to be some anomaly, but it will take a good deal of careful toothbrushing before anything is known for certain. If you can spare an hour from your own research, Miguel and his crew will certainly appreciate your unskilled labor. See him and sign up. I guess that's all."

I just followed the slim stream of other volunteers. Hell, I nearly busted my copious buns getting over there. Like this was a chance to get out of the dome and cruise the surface of the *moon*, right? You don't have to twist *my* arm twice. So all the rest of the people are uniformed in white outfits with nametags, and I'm in leathers, chain mail, and hefting a saber and broadsword. But the only person who looked at me weird was Miguel himself, and he only made a quick little frown, then shrugged and put my name on his list. I don't know, maybe he thought the saber was like a long, thin slide rule or something.

Picture me kicking up a little moon dust, hopping around and getting an earthtan. I planned what I was going to say: "This is one small step for Maureen Birnbaum, like a giant *leap* for, you know, Maureen Birnbaum." But when the time came, I forgot. The moon is just *slightly* awesome. Dead, gray, and *filthy*, but awesome. I was *supposed* to have my own spacesuit, but like I didn't, so I "borrowed" one. I hoped the real owner wouldn't need it for anything while I was using it. I didn't have all *that* much concern for the real owner, 'cause like the inside of that suit smelled like the ladies' room of some grody stable preserved in *muck* for a hundred years.

Oh, I found out that I couldn't wear Old Betsy inside the spacesuit. I felt like whoa nelly! naked without her.

Miguel let us get our bearings, but like the closest to bearings *I* ever got was "up, down, here, there." Miguel held this big old chart and pointed. "Due north," I heard him go in my helmet radio. We booked it maybe a couple hundred yards, then Miguel goes, "All right." I couldn't see any way he could tell we were where we were supposed to be, but he had the map and I didn't. Still, all the holes in the ground and all the chunks of rock looked the same to me. Well, *I'm* not a scientist. They probably had names for *all* those chunks of rock. Like Larry and Curly and Moe and Whitney Houston or something.

So like I see right off what the "anomaly" was, and all the rest of us volunteers saw it, too, and we all went like *"Yipe!"* It looked like mondo cruddy remains of an old, old campsite, like those prehistoric men left all over Earth. But this was the *moon*, right? I wanted to ask Miguel what the hell it was *doing* here, but Miguel probably didn't know, either. There were burnt-out campfires and piles of megaold garbage, broken up pots and things, even bones and skulls, and these spazzy drawings and markings. We all were, you know, stunned and speechless and all, and we didn't have Idea One about what to do next. So we did what Colonel Jennings said: we spent the hour going through the moon dust with toothbrushes, and making no particular progress at all. I decided that come "nightfall," when all the good little scientists were tucked in, I was going to come out here by myself and look around. I mean, I didn't have a dorm room or anything, I was going to have to sleep in the *cafeteria.* Which is what I did. Go out and look around by *myself,* I mean.

The next morning, the L.I.F.E. people ate breakfast and got to their tasks. Colonel Jennings asked again for volunteers to sort out the anomaly, and like I wasn't doing anything *else* so I figured okay, I'd help. I climbed into another spacesuit—and believe *me,* the second one wasn't any sweeter-smelling than the first. What we need, I think, is a lemon-fresh-ened space program—and trundled out to the digs like one of the Seven Dwarfs. Our fearless leader, Miguel, came to a sudden stop when we got there. He just stared for a long while, muttering angry-sounding Spanish things into his open microphone. Then there was a little peace, and finally an *explosion:* "Who had the goddamned *nerve* to come out here and screw up the greatest scientific find of the twenty-first *century?"*

I figured the twenty-first century was only like nineteen years *old*, right? There'd be plenty of time to have *another* great scientific find somewhere else.

Everybody just stood there, shocked or embarrassed or angry. Miguel glared from one of us to another. After a while, my innate honesty and the Code of Champions required that I like raise my hand. *"I did it,"* I go. All the other spacesuits turned to look at me. I felt like *so* bagged out.

"And who are *you?"* Miguel goes.

"Maureen Danielle Birnbaum," I go.

"What department?"

I thought fast. "Security," I go.

"And you don't know a damn thing about the proper procedure to pre- serve and study an ancient habitation site such as this. You should have stuck to your field of expertise. Why couldn't you have let the work be done by people who've been *trained* for it?" I didn't want to mention that like we didn't *have* any of those with us on the moon.

Well, okay, like I *mentioned* it, really quiet, though.

"We *do* have photographers. We could have laid the groundwork for a more specialized and better-prepared team."

"Yeah," I go, "I guess so."

Everybody moved closer to the site to see like what I'd done. Yesterday there had been these *yucky* heaps of body parts, mounds of half-eaten creatures—mostly bone but with some dried stuff still clinging to them, on account of millions of years without air—and these puny old weapons that like couldn't cut through a soggy rabbit or *anything*. I had cleared the bones away real nice, carted off the trash piles, and tossed it all into some deep old craters a little ways away, out of sight. I thought I'd improved the cheerfulness of the whole neighborhood.

One of the volunteers goes, "Now it looks like some shabby slum dwell- ing on a hillside above Rio."

I didn't buy that, 'cause like I'd brought out decorative stuff from the mission dormitory building. I put dried straw flowers into two rude, mud native bowls. I hung up reproductions of famous paintings—Van Gogh's *Sunflowers* and a Degas ballet thing and something by Magritte. The whole site was now nice and clean and livable. Maybe it *was* a scientific goof, I don't know. I'm just a fighting woman.

"Why, why, *why?"* goes Miguel. "Have you no concept of the *tragedy* you've caused here, of the *humiliation* we'll all have to face when the world hears about this?"

152

"Hey," I go, "like I'm *real* sorry, all right?"

"No," he goes, "it *isn't* all right."

"I just got rid of all that useless, broken, discarded junk. I don't see what you're so all-fired *angry* about. What *good* was it all? We have *better* discarded junk on Earth, just *tons* of it. It was just ugly, pointless grunge."

"Ugly? Pointless?" Miguel goes. "Don't you know the first axiom in the study of a new primitive society? These items are *clues* to their entire culture. Where the hell did you go to school? Didn't anybody ever teach you that mess is lore?"

Mess is lore, I'm so sure.

That did it. I just turned my back and stomped toward the dome in regal silence. Perfect posture, icy *hauteur,* all that superior stuff. I passed through the airlock, stripped off that skanky spacesuit, and kissed off the moon forever. I whooshed myself right out of there, like I didn't care *who* saw me go.

I WAS SITTING across the desk from some junior executive type, who was studying me as if I were a couple of long blonde hairs on his poached egg. He didn't seem happy, but I guess that's what he was paid for. He goes, "Why do you think assembling our Pocket Fisherman is the right job for you?"

I was going to tell him that it was a job any idiot could do with his brain turned off, but I really needed to have an income and I didn't care what I did. I go, "Well, sir, I'm sure that—"

That's when Muffy burst in. She'd left the spacesuit outside, but she still made quite a first impression in her warrior-woman garb and the goddamn broadsword. "Listen here, pal," she goes, marching right up to the guy's desk. "Bitsy is a modern woman who has taken charge of her life. She's capable of filling any position in this monkey ranch, including yours. I just want to make sure—"

The executive looked at me. "Friend of yours?" he goes.

"Yes," I go. "Forgive her. She's a little enthusiastic sometimes."

Maureen whanged his desk with Old Betsy. He didn't like that. "She get the job or no?" she goes.

He looked at me again. "What exactly is your relationship to her? If she's not your patient, I probably don't want to hear it."

"Just friends," I go, kind of meekly.

Muffy held the sword with the point aimed directly at the guy's heart.

"I said, does she get the job?"

"Sorry," the executive goes, *"the position's already been filled. We'll keep your application on file, of course. Please leave now."*

Muffy raged. "Just a minute, you weaselly little—"

I stood up and got the hell out of there. For all I know, Maureen stayed behind and made Junior Executive Szechuan Style out of the poor man.

I got to my car and drove home.

And I've been living in terror of her return ever since. Wouldn't you?